THE ENEMIES
OF JUPITER

THE ROMAN MYSTERIES
by Caroline Lawrence

—— A Roman Mystery ——

THE ENEMIES
OF JUPITER

Caroline Lawrence

Orion
Children's Books

First published in Great Britain in 2003
by Orion Children's Books
a division of the Orion Publishing Group Ltd
Orion House
5 Upper St Martin's Lane
London WC2H 9EA

A catalogue record for this book is available
from the British Library.

ISBN 1 84255 251 1

Typeset at The Spartan Press Ltd,
Lymington, Hants
Printed in Great Britain by
Clays Ltd, St Ives plc

To Margaret A. Brucia, Ralph Jackson,
Nodge Nolan and Robert Wagman
with thanks for their help

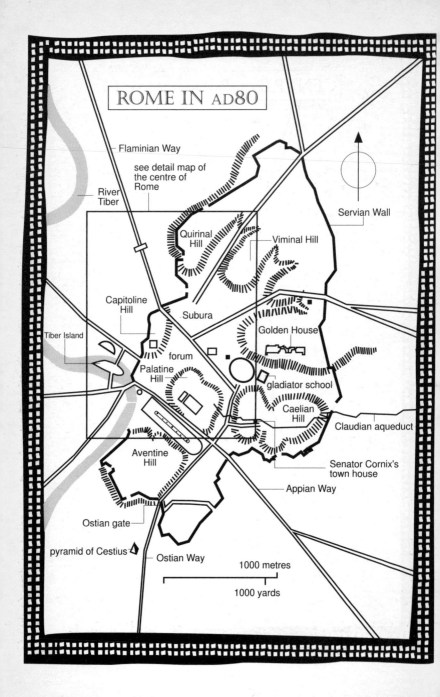

ROME IN AD80

Flaminian Way

see detail map of
the centre of
Rome

River
Tiber

Servian Wall

Quirinal
Hill

Viminal Hill

Capitoline
Hill

Subura

Tiber Island

Golden House

forum

Palatine
Hill

gladiator school

Caelian
Hill

Claudian aqueduct

Aventine
Hill

Senator Cornix's
town house

Ostian gate

Appian Way

pyramid of Cestius

Ostian Way

1000 metres

1000 yards

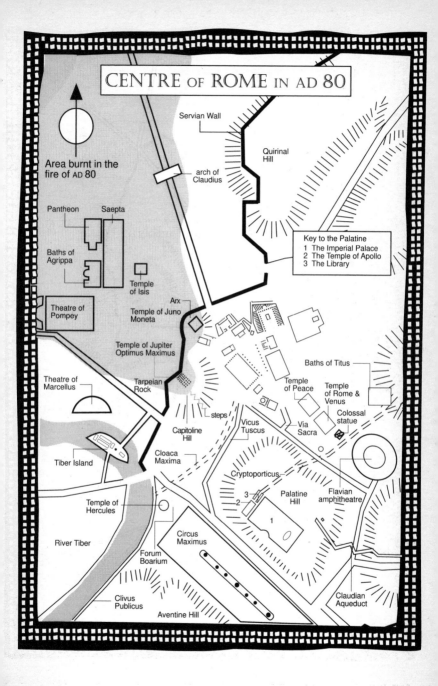

CENTRE OF ROME IN AD 80

Area burnt in the fire of AD 80

Servian Wall

Quirinal Hill

arch of Claudius

Key to the Palatine
1 The Imperial Palace
2 The Temple of Apollo
3 The Library

Pantheon

Saepta

Baths of Agrippa

Temple of Isis

Arx

Theatre of Pompey

Temple of Juno Moneta

Temple of Jupiter Optimus Maximus

Baths of Titus

Temple of Peace

Temple of Rome & Venus

Tarpeian Rock

Theatre of Marcellus

steps

Capitoline Hill

Vicus Tuscus

Via Sacra

Colossal statue

Tiber Island

Cloaca Maxima

Cryptoporticus

Flavian amphitheatre

Temple of Hercules

3

2

Palatine Hill

1

River Tiber

Forum Boarium

Circus Maximus

Clivus Publicus

Aventine Hill

Claudian Aqueduct

This story takes place in Ancient Roman times, so a few of the words and names may look strange.

If you don't know them, 'Aristo's Scroll' at the back of the book will tell you what they mean and how to pronounce them. It will also tell you a little about the real and mythological characters mentioned in this book.

SCROLL I

Jonathan ben Mordecai stared at the charred flesh.

'It's horrible,' he said to his friend Lupus in a strangled voice. 'Horrible.'

Lupus could not speak because he had no tongue. So he merely nodded.

The two boys were crouching before a brick oven and peering in through the arched doorway. A blackened haunch of venison lay on a platter among the glowing coals.

'Do you think maybe I left it in too long?' asked Jonathan.

Lupus nodded again.

Using a napkin, Jonathan gripped the platter and began to pull it out.

'Yeoww! It's hot!'

There was a resounding crash and Jonathan stared down at burnt meat and broken pottery on the concrete floor of the kitchen.

'Oh Pollux!' Jonathan cursed and blew on his scorched fingers. 'Now dinner is completely ruined. And it's all Miriam's fault!'

Lupus stared at Jonathan with raised eyebrows.

'Well it is! Everything's gone wrong since she got married and left home!' Jonathan stood up and tried to blink away the tears filling his eyes, so he could read what Lupus was beginning to write on his wax tablet.

YOU COULD SCRAPE

But before Lupus could finish, a big black puppy pushed between his legs, seized the burnt leg of venison in his teeth and scampered back out of the kitchen.

'Tigris! Bad dog! Come back with that!' yelled Jonathan. 'That's father's birthday dinner! Oh Pollux!' he cursed again. 'This is a total disaster. It's going to be even worse than your birthday party last week. At least we had food, even if it was burnt.'

Lupus nodded, then shrugged and pointed to his tongueless mouth, as if to say: I couldn't taste it anyway.

Jonathan gave his friend an affectionate glance. Less than a year ago Lupus had been a half-wild beggar boy with head lice and ragged fingernails. Now, with his hair oiled and combed, wearing a white birthday tunic, he looked like a young Roman boy of good birth.

From the direction of the atrium came the sound of the door knocker.

'That must be father,' said Jonathan. 'He probably forgot his key again. He's just in time for the total disaster that's supposed to be his birthday party. Could you let him in, Lupus? I'll start picking up these broken pieces of pottery before one of us steps on them and bleeds to death.'

A moment later Lupus was back, followed by a dark-skinned girl in a lionskin cloak and a fair-haired girl wearing a blue palla. Behind them came two adult slaves: a plump woman and a big muscular man carrying a covered cauldron.

'Salve, Jonathan!' said the dark-skinned girl, and the girl with light brown hair said: 'What happened?'

'Oh, hello, Nubia. Hello, Flavia. I dropped father's birthday dinner and Tigris ran off with it and it's a total disaster.'

'Don't be wretched,' said Nubia, the dark-skinned girl. The rear paws of her lionskin trailed on the floor as she knelt to help Jonathan pick up the shards of clay.

Flavia grinned down at Jonathan. 'After Lupus's party last week,' she said, 'we thought you might need some help with the cooking. So Alma made her special goat stew with plums and pine-nuts. Caudex will help serve it.' Flavia stepped out of the kitchen into the columned peristyle. She looked around the inner garden. 'Where's your father?' she asked, tapping a cylindrical package against her leg. 'We have a present for him.'

'He's not back yet,' said Jonathan. 'He's still out seeing his patients. Thanks, Alma.' This last was addressed to the plump woman who was settling the cauldron among the glowing ashes on top of the hearth.

'My pleasure, dear.' Alma turned to hang her cloak on a peg fixed to the wall behind her. 'Why don't you four go and tidy the dining room? Leave the kitchen to Caudex and me. We'll get everything ready. If one of you could just bring a broom, Caudex can sweep up these shards of clay.'

Beside her, Flavia's big door-slave yawned and nodded.

'It's a mess in here, too,' said Flavia to Jonathan a few minutes later as they entered the dining room.

'Your house is not being of the tidy,' Nubia agreed. She had only been in Italia for eight months and her Latin was not yet fluent.

'I know,' Jonathan said. He had taken a piece of flatbread from the kitchen and now he tore off a chunk with his teeth. 'Cleaning is usually my job but I've had to be the cook, too, since Miriam left. Sometimes we get dinner from the tavern by the Baths of Thetis, but the food is nowhere near as good as Miriam's. I wish father would let us keep slaves – oh, sorry, Nubia! I forgot you used to be a slave.'

'I do not mind,' said Nubia. She plumped one of the embroidered floor cushions. 'I am not a slave any more.'

'I'm glad we have slaves to do all the chores,' said Flavia, as she brushed crumbs from the low hexagonal table in the middle of the dining room. 'I don't know how we'd manage without Alma and Caudex. It's a shame your father has such strange ideas.'

Behind them, Lupus was lighting hanging oil-lamps with a thin taper. It was a late afternoon in February and already the light was draining from the sky.

'And that's another thing,' said Jonathan through his mouthful. 'It's the Sabbath and there should be a woman to light the candles.' He gestured with his bread at the unlit candles on the table. 'And to say the blessing.'

'Maybe Miriam can say it when she gets here,' said Flavia. 'I can't wait to see her!'

'She's not coming,' said Jonathan.

'But it is your father's birthday!' said Nubia.

'She hasn't had the fever. Neither has Gaius. Father sent them a message telling them not to come into Ostia until the epidemic is over.'

Flavia and Nubia exchanged a glance. 'But we haven't seen her or Gaius since the wedding last month,' said Flavia. 'We really wanted to see them.'

'I know.' Jonathan sighed. 'I miss her, too.'

'Stew's ready,' said Alma, putting her head into the dining room. 'Shall I bring it in?'

'Not yet,' said Flavia. 'The guest of honour still isn't back. Where could your father be?' she asked. 'It's almost dark.'

'He's out tending the sick,' said Jonathan. 'As usual.'

'He tends sick on the birthday?' asked Nubia.

'Yes,' sighed Jonathan. 'Though he's usually back by dusk on the Sabbath.'

Flavia's eyes grew wide. 'You don't think he's caught the fever, do you?'

'Probably,' said Jonathan. 'In fact, I'm amazed he hasn't caught it before now. He's probably lying in a gutter somewhere, moaning for his loved ones . . .'

'Who's lying in a gutter?' said an accented voice.

'Father!' Jonathan spun round. And then: 'Father?'

A tall, clean-shaven Roman in a white tunic stood in the doorway of the dining room. His heavy-lidded dark eyes gleamed with amusement.

Jonathan's jaw dropped. 'Great Neptune's beard, father! What have you done to yourself?'

SCROLL II

'Doctor Mordecai!' gasped Flavia. 'You look just like a Roman.'

'Behold!' said Nubia. 'You have cut your hairs.'

With his forefinger, Lupus pretended to shave his own smooth cheeks.

'And shaved off your beard!' agreed Jonathan. 'Great Jupiter's eyebrows, father! Why did you do that?'

'I have a growing number of Roman patients,' said his father with a sigh, 'who prefer a "Roman-looking" doctor. Besides,' he added, 'since you saved the Emperor Titus and he made us Roman citizens, I thought it was time I started looking like one!'

Later that night, Jonathan stared up into the dark shadowed ceiling of his bedroom. He couldn't sleep. Something he had overheard Alma say earlier that evening kept nagging at his thoughts.

He had been taking the wine jug into the kitchen for a refill just as she muttered to Caudex, 'There's only one reason I know for a forty-three-year-old man to change his looks like that and it's not Roman citizenship. I'll wager he's got a new woman in his life.'

Alma had looked up to see Jonathan standing in the kitchen doorway and she had furiously shushed poor Caudex, although the big door-slave hadn't said a word.

Now Jonathan was wondering whether Alma was right. A few months earlier Flavia's father had almost taken a new wife. What if his father was thinking of remarrying as well?

The brand on Jonathan's left shoulder began to throb, so he rolled onto his good side.

'You *can't* have a new woman in your life, father,' he murmured. 'Mother's still alive and well and living in Rome, less than fifteen miles away.'

He reached out and touched the plaster-covered wall inches from his nose. The surface was silky smooth and slightly damp on this winter night. His finger found a rough edge, where the plaster had cracked, and he absently picked at it.

'If only she hadn't made me promise not to tell you.'

Something woke Lupus.

For a moment he tried to remember his dream. He had been swimming with dolphins in water so clear that it felt like flying.

His ear caught the remote clatter of the fire-gong somewhere near the harbour, and the distant sound of dogs barking. Was that what had woken him? No, that was a common sound on winter nights. He listened as hard as a rabbit for something closer. There! The soft grating of wooden chair legs on a mosaic floor. Someone was downstairs in the study.

For a moment Lupus hesitated. It was a cold night and he was deliciously warm in his burrow of soft blankets. Abruptly he laughed at himself. This time last year he would have been sleeping half-naked near the furnace in the Baths of Thetis, trying to find some warmth in the cooling ashes. How soft he had grown in the last eight months!

Lupus lifted himself on one elbow. The tiny flame of a night oil-lamp in one corner showed that both Jonathan and Tigris were gone.

Lupus rose from his warm bed and padded across the cold bedroom floor onto the balcony overlooking the inner garden of the house. The bare branches of the fig tree made it easy to see down through the columns of the peristyle. The gauzy curtains of the study were drawn, but a lamp shining behind illuminated them with a golden glow.

Slowly Lupus crept downstairs, avoiding the squeaky third step from the top. Presently his bare feet felt the cold roughness of the mosaic path with its diamond pattern of white chips, barely visible on this moonless night.

When Lupus reached the study, he peeked through a gap between the edge of the wide doorway and the curtain pulled across it.

The light from the oil-lamp showed Jonathan – a blanket wrapped round his shoulders – sitting at his father's desk. He held a half-eaten apple in his left hand and a quill pen in his right and, as Lupus watched, he dipped the pen into a blue glass inkpot on the desk before him and wrote carefully on a piece of papyrus.

Something moved under the desk. It was Tigris,

gnawing the bone from the leg of venison he had stolen earlier.

Lupus watched Jonathan replace the pen, blow on the sheet, re-read it, and fold it. Another letter lay on the desk beside him. Finally, Jonathan lit the special red wax taper his father used to seal letters and dripped wax onto the edge of the papyrus where it overlapped.

Lupus stifled a grunt of surprise as he saw Jonathan press the liquid wax with a ring on the middle finger of his right hand. The only ring Jonathan wore on that hand was a signet ring which had been a gift to him from the Emperor Titus.

Lupus also knew that the seal carved into the ring was not Jonathan's.

It was the Emperor's.

'Father,' said Jonathan two days later, 'would you like me to help you receive your patients today?'

It was the first day of the week, which they called the Lord's day.

Jonathan, Mordecai and Lupus had just returned from their pre-dawn meeting with the other followers of the new Jewish sect who called themselves Christians.

Now Mordecai was standing over his desk, grinding cardamoms with a mortar and pestle made of dark green marble. He stopped and looked up at Jonathan.

'Don't you have lessons with Aristo this morning?'

Jonathan shook his head. 'Flavia's household are observing the first day of the Parentalia. Except for Aristo. He and Lupus are going hunting. I know you've been busy these past few weeks and you haven't had Miriam to help you and I thought you could use some help.'

'That is extremely thoughtful of you,' said his father. 'I would greatly appreciate your assistance.'

Jonathan was surprised by the look of gratitude on his father's face and turned quickly to hide the guilty expression on his own. His real motive for helping his father was to see if any suspicious women patients appeared. Especially ones who preferred a clean-shaven Roman to a bearded Jew.

'Will you open the front door?' said his father. 'Show the patients into the atrium as usual and bring the first one in.'

'Yes, father.' Jonathan went into the atrium and unbolted the front door.

It had been a long time since he had helped his father receive patients and he was surprised to see there were already a dozen of them waiting on the pavement outside. And most of them were women.

SCROLL III

Jonathan studied his father's last patient of the day, a plump woman with a little red mouth and dark brown hair arranged in the latest fashion: a wall of curls rising up above her forehead. She looked up at Jonathan from her chair and smiled at him.

'You've met my son Jonathan?' said Mordecai. 'He's assisting me today. Jonathan, this is Helena Aurelia.'

'Hello, Jonathan,' she said. 'I was just telling Marcus how much I like his new look.'

'Marcus? Who's Marcus?' Jonathan frowned.

'Your father.'

'His name is Mordecai,' said Jonathan coldly.

'Oh!' cried Helena, 'I can never pronounce that name. I always call him Marcus.' She had such a pretty laugh that Jonathan smiled despite himself.

'Tell me, Helena Aurelia,' said Jonathan's father, smiling too. 'What is bothering you?'

'It's the usual thing, Marcus. I can't sleep. My mind is racing. I'm forgetful. And I become very frightened for no reason.' She looked up at Mordecai from under long eyelashes. 'My husband died two years ago and we have no children. Apart from the slaves, I'm all alone in that big house.'

Jonathan's father nodded. 'Show me your tongue please, domina.'

Helena obligingly stuck out her tongue.

'Just turn towards the garden, the light's better there . . . Thank you. You can close your mouth now.'

Jonathan watched her with narrowed eyes.

'Well, Jonathan,' said his father, looking over at him. 'What do you think?'

'Me?' Jonathan was surprised. 'You want to know what I think?'

'I do. The patient's tongue and colour are fine. You heard her complaint. What's your opinion?'

'She probably has an excess of vicious humours.'

His father nodded. 'Treatment?'

'Bleed her,' said Jonathan with relish, and then added, 'and a tonic might help.'

'Which tonic?' asked Mordecai.

'Either *hydromel* or the special elixir.'

'Special elixir?' Helena's eyes lit up.

'I hadn't thought of that,' said Mordecai, reaching up to stroke his beard. Jonathan saw the look of surprise flash across his father's face as his hand encountered a beardless chin.

'Oh, Marcus!' cried Helena. 'You never told me there was a special elixir. I want it!'

'It's not cheap . . .' said Mordecai.

'I'll pay any price!'

'Very well. I'll prepare some as soon as we've bled you. I think I have most of the ingredients here . . . Jonathan, can you go to my cabinet upstairs and bring me some poppy-tears, turpentine and honey?'

'Um . . . I don't think there's any honey left.'

His father turned, frowning. 'What do you mean? Just last week one of my patients paid me with a large jar of the finest Hymettan honey.'

'It's gone.'

'Already? But how?'

Jonathan hung his head. 'I ate it.'

'You ate it? You ate an entire jar of honey?'

Helena laughed her silvery laugh and this time Jonathan shot her a glare.

'I just wanted a little taste,' he said to his father. 'And then I went back for another and . . . I'm sorry.'

Helena was still laughing and Mordecai tried not to smile. 'Thank you for telling me,' he said, 'I appreciate your honesty. But honey isn't just food: it's medicine!'

'I know,' said Jonathan. He didn't tell his father that food was the only thing that seemed to fill the empty ache inside him.

'Did you devour the sugar, too?' said his father dryly.

'Sugar? What's that?'

'The sugar loaf is the large greyish-white cylinder in the medicine cabinet of the upstairs storeroom. Be careful, Jonathan, it's extremely expensive and rare.'

'I'll get it,' said Jonathan and a few moments later he carried an object as long as his forearm back into the atrium. It looked like a big marble pestle, so he was astonished to see his father take a scalpel and scrape a small amount of white powder from its surface onto a piece of papyrus.

'Hold out your hands.'

Both Helena and Jonathan obligingly held out their

hands and Mordecai sprinkled a little powder into the palm of each.

'Taste it,' said Mordecai, with a smile.

'Mmmm,' said Jonathan.

'It's delicious!' Helena giggled. She licked her small red lips and batted her eyelashes at Jonathan's father. 'Almost as sweet as you are, Marcus.'

'Helena Aurelia. She's the one to watch,' growled Jonathan, as he and Lupus stepped through Flavia's door into the atrium. It was shortly past dawn on the following day. 'I'm sure she's after father. She's always – Great Jupiter's eyebrows! What are those?'

'Those are the death masks of my family ancestors.' Flavia led the boys around the rainwater pool to the family shrine. The lararium was a wooden cupboard with a miniature temple on top. Usually the red and blue doors were shut but today they were wide open, revealing painted beeswax masks of men and women.

'They look so real,' said Jonathan with a shudder. He counted fourteen of them. Six on the central shelves and four hanging on the inside of each door.

Lupus was writing on his wax tablet:

DEATH MASKS?!

'Yes,' said Flavia quietly. 'Whenever one of my family dies they make a mould of their face with plaster, then pour in beeswax and paint it. We bring them out during the festival of the Parentalia to show them reverence. And on the last day we go to the tombs.'

Lupus pointed at the mask of a fierce-looking old man and raised his eyebrows questioningly at Flavia.

'That's my great-grandfather, the first one of our branch of the family to come to Ostia. He grew up in the north of Italia. I never knew him. After he moved here, he made his fortune trading salt. Later he bought the farm in Stabia.' After a moment she pointed. 'That's my mother.'

'She looks like you,' said Jonathan. 'Was her hair really that dark?'

Flavia nodded. 'I get my fair hair from pater.' She gazed at the mask for a moment and then turned away. 'Come on,' she said. 'Let's sit at the table. It's almost time for lessons and I want to look over the passage before Aristo comes down.'

'Can't we have our lessons somewhere else today?' Jonathan shot an uneasy glance towards the lararium. 'Those death masks are spooky!'

'*Memento mori*. Alma says it's good to be reminded that one day we will all die. It helps us live every day as if it were our last.'

'What a cheerful thought to start the day with,' said Jonathan, and then added, 'but if it's all the same to you, I'll sit with my back to the death masks this morning.'

'Tragedy,' said Aristo, 'touches the lives of us all. None of us is immune.'

He sat at one end of the oval table and looked round at his four pupils. The deep Egyptian blue of the plaster wall behind him made his face look pale. And not for the first time, Nubia noticed shadows under his eyes. She knew that her handsome tutor was still hopelessly in love with Jonathan's sister.

Nubia wondered if Aristo thought his own life was tragic.

'We Greeks,' he continued, 'are famous for our tragedies. The heroes of our plays aren't just sad at the end. They are destroyed. If they aren't dead, they wish they were.'

'Why do the Greeks write such sad plays?' asked Flavia. 'It's so depressing.'

Lupus grunted his agreement.

'When we read a tragedy,' said Aristo, 'or watch one at the theatre, we see people whose lives are much worse than ours. And somehow that brings us comfort. My life may be hard, I may suffer, but at least I didn't murder my father, marry my mother, and stab out my eyes like Oedipus.'

Jonathan snorted. 'The next time I'm sad, I'll read about a man who murders his father, marries his mother and stabs out his own eyes. Then I'll feel *much* better.'

'Be as sarcastic as you like,' said Aristo, 'but it's true. I've seen people go away from a tragic play encouraged, comforted, even uplifted.' He leaned forward, resting his elbows on the polished walnut surface of the table. 'But tragedy serves another purpose. It warns us about hubris.'

'What is who bricks?' asked Nubia.

'Bris, not bricks. Hubris. The word means over-weening pride. Presumption. Insolence. Towards other people but especially towards the gods.'

'Overweening?' said Nubia.

'Let me illustrate it with an example. Do you know who Medusa is?'

Nubia smiled and nodded: here was something she knew. 'Medusa is a horrible monster-woman,' she said, 'having snakes for hairs and is turning men to stone by her ugly face. Perseus cuts off her head and puts it in a bag.'

'Yes, but did you know that she wasn't always ugly? Once she was the most beautiful woman on earth. But one day she boasted that her beauty was greater than Venus's—'

'Uh-oh,' said Flavia. 'You should never, *ever* boast if it concerns the gods.'

'Yes,' agreed Jonathan. 'Those naughty gods will turn you into a spider or a slug before you can blink.'

'Thank you for that demonstration of mild hubris, Jonathan,' said Aristo dryly. 'Would you care to take it up a notch?'

'I don't even believe in your gods,' Jonathan snorted. 'They're just a bunch of made-up stories.'

'That will do nicely.'

'Doctor Mordecai,' Flavia asked casually, as they ate dinner together later that afternoon. 'How did you meet Jonathan's mother? Was your marriage arranged? Or did you marry for love? I don't want to be rude, but I'm going to be betrothed soon and I was just wondering . . .' she trailed off and glanced at Jonathan. He had confided his fears to her and she had agreed to help him get more information. Love and marriage were subjects his father found painful to talk about, but he just might reply to a direct question from a guest.

Flavia saw Jonathan give her the merest nod of thanks and then pretend to be more interested in dipping a scrap of bread in the stew.

Mordecai put his wine cup down on the hexagonal table and stared into the pink liquid.

They all held their breath.

'It must have been sixteen years ago, now,' he said at last. 'A perfect spring evening in Jerusalem. I was walking down a street between the Joppa Gate and the Spice Market and I heard laughter – a girl's laughter. It came from an inner courtyard. I stopped. She laughed again and – this sounds ridiculous – I somehow knew that I was to marry her.'

'Oh!' cried Flavia. 'That's so romantic!'

'But you do not know if she is being old or ugly!' said Nubia, her eyes wide with amazement.

'The thought never occurred to me,' he said with a faint smile. 'I went back every evening at the same time. There was a palm tree on the street near her house. I used to stand beneath it, waiting for that laugh. I discovered that a priest owned the house, and that he had a daughter of marriageable age. I went through the proper channels, asked for her hand in marriage, and he agreed.'

Flavia wiggled her eyebrows at Nubia, who covered a giggle with her hand.

But Jonathan had a strange look on his face. 'You fell in love with my mother's laugh?' he asked.

Mordecai nodded. 'It was a beautiful, silvery laugh,

and so infectious . . . The first time I heard it, I knew I could love her.'

'And when you saw her for the first time, you must have fallen in love even more,' sighed Flavia.

Mordecai nodded again. He had a faraway look in his eyes.

Tigris lifted his head from his lamb-bone, uttered a single bark and ran out of the dining room. Lupus followed him and a moment later they heard a knock on the door.

'Who could it be at this hour?' said Jonathan with a scowl.

Presently Lupus reappeared with a scrawny slave.

'My mistress,' said the slave in a meek voice, 'apologises for the hour of this visit but she is in urgent need of the doctor's services and begs him to come to her home on Mulberry Street.'

'Who is your mistress?' asked Mordecai, rising to his feet.

'Helena Aurelia,' said the slave. And added, 'She says it's an emergency.'

SCROLL IV

'Emergency my big toe!' Lupus heard Jonathan mutter at the sound of the front door closing. 'Her only emergency is finding a new husband.'

'At least we know she's not just after his money,' said Flavia. 'Alma says Helena Aurelia is very wealthy because her husband left her a warehouse full of rope and tar and sailcloth and other ships' tackle.'

Lupus nodded his agreement. He had heard similar rumours in the markets.

'I should have bled her dry this morning!' growled Jonathan.

Lupus opened his eyes wide. He had helped Mordecai bleed patients on occasion but had only been allowed to hold the cup. He pointed at Jonathan as if to say: *you*?

'Yes, me,' said Jonathan, lifting his chin a little. 'It was the first time he's let me make the cut.' Then his shoulders slumped. 'Now that Miriam's gone I suppose he'll train me to be his assistant.'

'What is bleed?' Nubia stopped stroking Tigris, who had just come in from the inner garden.

'Don't you know?' Jonathan looked surprised.

Lupus ran out of the room, opened the cabinet in Mordecai's study and found a cupping vessel. A few moments later he handed it to Nubia.

'It is smooth and bronze and is looking like a big goat-bell.' Nubia shook it and frowned. 'But with no bell noise.' She peered inside.

Lupus nodded to say: That's what I thought at first, too.

Nubia let Tigris sniff the cup. He sneezed and they all laughed.

'It's a cupping vessel,' said Jonathan. 'You make a cut in someone's arm so that the blood starts to flow. But the blood would stop after a minute if you left it alone. So you take a piece of lighted papyrus or lint . . .'

Here Lupus fished in his belt pouch and produced a scrap of papyrus. He held it to one of the coals in the brazier and when it caught fire, he dropped the flaming scrap into the bronze bell. Immediately, he applied the open end of the cup to the soft underside of his upper arm.

'Does it not burn?' asked Nubia.

Lupus grinned and shook his head. He felt the warmth and the pleasant suction as the cupping vessel adhered.

'It doesn't hurt,' Jonathan confirmed. 'The fire goes out the moment you press it to the skin and it makes a vacuum which sucks out the blood. Or the vicious humours if you haven't made a cut. Look!' He pointed at Lupus, who stood with his arm extended.

Lupus took his hand away to let the heavy bronze cup hang from his arm. He grinned at Nubia's look of amazement. She tentatively reached for it. The smooth bronze cup came away with a satisfying sucking sound.

'Where are the vicious humours?' She peered into the cup.

'You can't see them,' said Jonathan. 'They're invisible. You can see blood, of course, but not the vicious humours.'

Nubia let Tigris sniff the cup again. This time he wagged his tail.

'What are vicious humours anyway?' asked Flavia, feeding Tigris a piece of gravy-soaked flatbread. 'I've heard of them, of course. Everyone has. But I don't really understand what they are.'

'Each of us tends to have too much of one of the four humours,' said Jonathan. 'For example, according to father, Lupus is phlegmatic. That means his brain produces too much phlegm sometimes.'

'Flem?' said Nubia.

'The stuff that comes out of your nose?' said Flavia.

Lupus nodded proudly. He was writing on his tablet:

PHLEGM MAKES YOU BRAVE
WARRIORS DRINK IT

'I don't believe you,' said Flavia.

'It's true,' said Jonathan. 'According to father, some Greek soldiers used to drink a mixture of bull and goat mucus before battles. It's called *snorteum*.'

'Ewww!' said Flavia, and then sat up straight. 'Do me! Which of the four humours do I have too much of? Maybe good humour?' She grinned.

Jonathan and Lupus looked at one another thoughtfully.

Then Lupus wrote:

SANGUINE!

'I think you're right, Lupus,' said Jonathan. 'Sanguine people have too much blood. Their cheeks are pink and they blush easily.'

'That's me,' said Flavia.

'They're quick at making decisions, even impetuous.'

'That's definitely me.'

'They're usually cheerful. Although they can be moody,' he added. 'Their season is spring and their element is air.'

'Why?'

'It just is.'

'I like being spring and air,' said Flavia. 'What's Nubia's type?'

Jonathan and Lupus looked at one another. Lupus shrugged, then wrote:

PHLEGMATIC LIKE ME?
OR MAYBE CHOLERIC

'What?' asked Nubia, frowning at the tablet. 'How do you know so much, Lupus?' said Flavia. 'I don't know any of that.'

Lupus shrugged. He liked helping Jonathan's father treat patients.

'Choleric people can be anxious or irritable,' Jonathan explained to Nubia. 'Their livers produce too much bile. Bile is a kind of thick yellow liquid.'

'Nubia's hardly ever irritable,' said Flavia. 'But you do get anxious sometimes, don't you?'

'Anxious?'

'Worried.'

'Yes,' said Nubia. 'I have overweening nightmares.'

'If Nubia's choleric,' said Flavia, 'then what's her element?'

FIRE wrote Lupus.

And Jonathan added, 'And her best season is summer.'

'I like summer,' said Nubia. 'When it is dry and hot. And I am born in the summer.'

'That doesn't really have anything to do with it,' said Jonathan. 'But I think you probably are choleric.'

'Are you flem attic, like Lupus?' Nubia asked Jonathan.

'No.' He sighed. 'According to father, I'm melancholic. That means my spleen tends to produce too much bile. But it's black bile, not yellow.'

'Ewww,' said Flavia.

THAT'S WHY HE'S DEPRESSED wrote Lupus.

'No,' said Jonathan slowly, as if speaking to Cletus the town idiot. 'The reason I'm depressed is because my mother would rather be in Rome with the Emperor than here with us.' And as Jonathan turned away Lupus was sure he heard him mutter: 'But I'm finally doing something about it.'

SCROLL V

The next day at noon, when Jonathan and Lupus came back from lessons at Flavia's house, they found a big soldier standing in Jonathan's atrium. He had just handed Mordecai a message and was trying to ignore Tigris's persistent barking. Jonathan's puppy was deeply suspicious of men who wore bright strips of metal.

'It's a message from the Emperor,' said Mordecai, glancing up at the boys. He thumbed off the wax seal, unfolded the papyrus and took it to the compluvium, where the light was best. Jonathan tried to look unconcerned, but his heart was racing. He and Lupus followed Mordecai. Tigris stopped barking and followed them, too.

'Titus says he has not forgotten the care I gave the people injured by the eruption of Vesuvius,' murmured Mordecai as he read the scroll, 'he has heard of my success in dealing with the fever here in Ostia . . . requests my medical expertise in Rome where the fever is killing hundreds every day . . . Dear Lord.' Mordecai absently refolded the message. 'I was afraid this might happen.'

'Will you go, father?' Jonathan's throat was dry and his heart still pounding.

Mordecai looked at his son from his heavy-lidded eyes.

'That man has the blood of ten thousand Jews on his hands,' he said in a very low voice. 'But I can hardly refuse a direct invitation from the Emperor, especially as he recently made me a Roman citizen.'

He turned back to the imperial messenger. 'Every stranger is an uninvited guest.' He bowed to the man. 'Please come in and take some refreshment.'

The soldier's armour clinked as he shook his head. 'I've a carriage waiting by the Roman Gate. The mules are being fed and watered. It would be best if we could leave as soon as you are ready, within the hour if possible.'

'Very well,' said Mordecai. 'We'll be there as soon as we can.' When he had closed the door behind the departing soldier he turned to the boys. 'You'd better get your things together,' he said, 'and don't forget to pack your musical instruments.'

'We're coming with you?' asked Jonathan, his heart still thumping.

Mordecai nodded. 'Flavia and Nubia, too,' he added, holding up the papyrus note. 'The Emperor has requested all four of you by name. Apparently he has a mystery he wants you to solve.'

'Pater, may Nubia and I go with Jonathan and Lupus to Rome?' Flavia sat on her father's knee and wrapped her arms round his neck.

Marcus Flavius Geminus put down his quill pen. 'I still can't imagine why the Emperor wants you and your friends up in Rome.'

'I told you how we saved his life a few months ago. He knows we're good at solving mysteries. And I suppose he trusts us.'

'What about the pestilence?'

'Doctor Mordecai says it's safe because we've already had the fever. Or at least I have. Nubia would have caught it by now if she was going to get it.'

Her father hesitated.

'We really want to go but if you say no I promise to obey you.'

'I appreciate your obedience.' Her father sighed and put down his pen. 'And because I myself must show obedience to the Emperor . . . Yes, you may go.'

Flavia squealed and hugged her father.

'Besides,' he said with a smile, 'I'm busy getting the *Delphina* ready for the sailing season. She needs a lot of work done if I'm to transform her from a slave-ship to a merchant ship and I could use Aristo's uninterrupted help.' Flavia kissed her father's cheek and noted with approval that he had been to the barber that morning. Recently he had begun skipping his daily visit, but today his cheek was smooth and the faint scent of his usual myrtle oil comforted her.

'Pater, do you promise to take winter violets and hyacinths to mater's tomb on the last day of the Parentalia if I'm not back? They were her favourites.'

'Of course,' he said, and patted her as she slid off his lap. 'And you must promise not to catch the fever again. Or to get into any trouble.'

'Don't worry, pater!' called Flavia, already on her

way upstairs to pack. 'I promise we won't get into any trouble at all!'

It was mid-afternoon when the imperial carriage began to pass tombs along the roadside, a sign that the city was not far off. Lupus caught the scent of imminent rain and – more faintly – the sweet smell of roasting meat. Among the tombs, cypress trees stood like tall dark flames which pointed accusingly up at the swollen sky. As the carriage topped a rise, Lupus saw something else. Something that had not been here the last time he came to Rome. Silhouetted against the grey sky were wooden crosses with men nailed to them. Three on each side of the road.

The men's naked bodies were covered with grime and blood and, as the carriage approached, Lupus saw that their faces were contorted in agony. A crow landed on the top of one cross and flapped its wings. With a thrill of horror Lupus saw the figure beneath it stir weakly: the men were still alive.

Lupus heard Mordecai murmur a prayer and Flavia whispered to Nubia:

'Probably runaway slaves. They've been crucified.'

'That is being crucified? Being nailed to wood?' Nubia's voice was barely audible.

'Yes,' Mordecai answered her. 'That's what they did to our Messiah, God's son.'

'They did that to your god?' Flavia sounded surprised.

'Yes. He allowed them to do it. He sacrificed himself for mankind.'

They were passing right below the crosses now and Lupus forced himself to look up. One of the crucified men had an open mouth which looked like a gaping wound. There was dried blood on his chin and throat and chest. Lupus knew with terrible certainty that the man's tongue had been cut out.

Abruptly, the imperial messenger twisted on his seat beside the driver. 'Close the flaps of the cover, would you?' he said. 'We're approaching Rome.' Lupus scowled. It wasn't raining and he wanted to see the piles of dead bodies everyone in Ostia had been talking about. But Mordecai was already following the messenger's instructions.

As Jonathan's father let the flaps fall shut, the interior of the carriage grew dim.

Lupus snorted with disgust. He wasn't going to sit in the dark. He had only been to Rome once before. And he wanted to catch another glimpse of the city as they entered it. He pushed the front flap aside and squeezed onto the bench between the messenger and the driver. The messenger frowned down at him, but the driver laughed and ruffled Lupus's hair.

Lupus endured this without snarling. If they allowed him to stay here then it was worth it.

They let him stay.

Now the carriage was moving between the graves of the rich. The winter sun had momentarily dropped beneath the clouds and it glazed the white tombs around them with a watery orange light. Lupus's nostrils flared: the scent of roast pork was stronger now. But when he saw plumes of dark smoke rising behind the graves, Lupus knew it wasn't pork he smelled. His throat contracted. Between the tombs he caught a brief glimpse of a dark body burning fiercely in the pale flames of a funeral pyre.

As they drew closer to Rome the graves became more impressive; these were the tombs of wealthy families. But the columns of smoke rising among them showed that the fever was striking down rich as well as poor.

Presently they passed beneath the pyramid-shaped tomb of Cestius, and now the three huge white arches of the Trigemina Gate lay before them. There were only a few carts and carrucas waiting outside. Lupus knew that most wheeled traffic was forbidden to enter Rome during the day, but the imperial carriage was an exception. The guards at the gate waved them through.

Lupus tipped his head back and watched the arch fill the sky above him and dim the world for a moment. Then the light grew brighter again as they came out the other side. Into Rome.

The big square with the fountain in the middle was almost deserted, but here and there people were scavenging among garbage heaps. Lupus looked again and grunted with satisfaction. What he had first taken for piles of clothes were dead and bloated bodies. Two soldiers were piling them onto carts. Beside Lupus, the messenger made the sign against evil. Lupus saw fear in his eyes.

But Lupus was not afraid. He had already had the fever and survived. The knowledge of that made him feel powerful. He noted with approval the envious gazes of two youths searching another pile of bodies for coins or jewellery. They must be wondering who he was: the boy in the sea-green tunic and fur-lined boots, sitting so proudly in the imperial carriage, obviously on his way to see the Emperor.

Presently the carriage emerged from between tall apartment blocks and the long Circus Maximus lay before them on the left. Beyond it rose the Palatine Hill, with the colourful columns and domes of the Imperial Palace partly screened by cypress, palms and umbrella pines.

Lupus sat up with interest. The broad street was suddenly full of people, mostly women and girls. Despite the heavy sky and the stench of death they seemed excited, even cheerful.

'Pollux!' cursed the messenger. 'I'd hoped we would avoid it.'

'No such luck,' growled the cart-driver.

'Imagine them coming out today.'

'I know,' said the driver, and added, 'my wife's probably here. As if we don't have enough mouths to feed already . . .'

'What is it?' Flavia's head pushed through the gap in the canvas and she peered over Lupus's shoulder.

'Today's the Lupercalia,' said the imperial messenger. 'The ceremony's not quite finished. You'd better get back inside. Here come the wolves.'

SCROLL VI

In the dim interior of the imperial carruca, Nubia shivered and pulled her lionskin cloak tighter round her shoulders.

She had been glad when they closed the flaps of the carriage. The sight of the men on their crosses and the terrible sweet scent of burning corpses had brought a deep sense of dread upon her. She wished she was back in Ostia. She and Flavia could be at the baths now, sitting in the hot laconicum with its resinated scent of baking pinewood.

Flavia was telling her about the Lupercalia, explaining that it was a festival for fertility, but Nubia wasn't listening. And she was only vaguely aware of the sound of women's shrieking laughter outside the carriage.

She was worried about Nipur. Would Alma remember to let him out for his afternoon romp in the woods?

Suddenly light flooded the interior of the carriage as one of the canvas flaps was thrown aside. Flavia squealed and Jonathan uttered an exclamation of surprise. Nubia looked up to see a blood-smeared teenager framed in the opening, naked apart from a leather loin-cloth and a wolfskin over his shoulders. The youth's laughing mouth was open and she could see his sharp little teeth and the whites of his eyes. He flicked some-

32

thing at Nubia and she flinched. Then he was gone and the carriage was dim again and everyone was looking at her. Nubia looked round at them and then down at herself.

She burst into tears.

Her precious lionskin cloak was spattered with bright red drops of fresh blood.

Flavia was trying to comfort Nubia. They had arrived at the Imperial Palace and their messenger had led them up a set of marble stairs to a suite of elegant rooms around a rectangular courtyard. A slave-girl had taken Nubia's cloak away to be cleaned.

But Nubia had found a spot of blood on the back of her hand and was washing it in the almond-shaped fountain at the centre of the courtyard.

'It won't hurt you, Nubia. It's just goat's blood. If it touches you it means you will be fruitful and have lots of babies. Most women want to be spattered by the wolf-boys. That's why they dressed up and came out even during the fever.'

But Nubia's golden eyes were full of tears now. They spilled over and wet her cheeks. She was shivering, too.

'Oh, Nubia!' Flavia put her arm around her friend's shoulder. 'Are you cold without your cloak? Here, come back into our room. Wrap this blanket around you. Look at the beautiful frescoes on our wall. They're the stories of Prometheus and Pandora. Do you want me to tell you?'

Nubia gave a little nod, but Flavia could feel her friend's shoulders still trembling under the soft blanket.

'Prometheus was a Titan,' began Flavia. 'One of the old gods that came before Jupiter, Juno, Minerva and all the other gods we have now. Prometheus brought fire down from Olympus because mankind didn't have fire and had to eat raw meat with the blood still in it. But Jupiter got angry with Prometheus. He didn't want man to have fire—'

'Why not?' whispered Nubia. 'Why did Jupiter not want man to have fire?'

'I'm not sure. Maybe because if man had fire he would be able to forge weapons and challenge the gods. Jupiter was so angry that he decided to punish Prometheus for bringing down fire and man for accepting it.'

Nubia had stopped trembling. 'How?' she whispered. 'How did he punish?'

'That panel shows how Jupiter punished man,' said Flavia. 'He did it by making a woman.'

'He punishes man with a woman?'

'Yes. Her name is Pandora. See how beautiful she is?'

Nubia nodded.

'Jupiter gave her a box full of hatred and envy and fear and disease and death.'

'Why? Why is he giving her a box with terrible things inside?'

'I'm not sure about that either. But in the story, Jupiter tells Pandora that she must never, ever open the box. Not under any circumstances. And of course she eventually does, because if you tell someone *not* to do something, well . . . that's all they think about doing. And when Pandora finally opens the box, she lets all the horrible things out into the world. Things like disease and death and grief.'

Flavia gestured towards the next panel.

'Pandora realises her mistake too late, and slams the lid shut. She's managed to trap one thing in the box. "Let me out," it cries. "I'm hope. Without me, people won't be able to bear the terrible things you've let loose!" At first Pandora doesn't believe it, but at last she does.'

'And is the one thing in the box really hope?'

'Yes,' said Flavia. 'Without hope we couldn't bear all the sadness and sickness in the world. And look at that panel! Jupiter is punishing Prometheus by chaining him to a column and sending a vulture to peck out his liver – that's one of the organs near your stomach. But because Prometheus is immortal and can't die, his liver grows back every night and then the vulture comes and pecks it out again during the day and he suffers unbearable pain forever.' Flavia pointed. 'See the drops of blood?'

Nubia nodded.

'There!' said Flavia, patting Nubia's back. 'Did that story cheer you up?'

Jonathan looked round the room he and Lupus were to share. It was next to the girls' room and he could hear Flavia's voice, though he couldn't make out her words. His father's room was across the courtyard; Mordecai had been unpacking his medical equipment when two imperial slaves had hurried him away to meet the other doctors.

Jonathan's heart was racing. At last. His father and mother were in the same city. Not only in the same city but within the same square mile. So close to one another that the distance could be measured in feet.

Lupus grunted at him, and Jonathan realised he'd been standing with a folded tunic in his hands for some moments.

'I'm all right,' he said in response to Lupus's questioning look. 'I was just thinking.' He put his spare tunic in the cedarwood box at the foot of his bed.

Lupus patted his bed and grinned at Jonathan.

'I know,' said Jonathan. 'Feather mattress. It's a bit too soft for me. I prefer a hard mattress.'

In response Lupus jumped onto his bed and sank into it, completely disappearing.

'Oh, look!' said Flavia, coming into the boys' room with Nubia. 'You've got the Sack of Troy on your walls.'

'I know what "sack" means,' said Nubia. 'It means the destroying of the town by warriors.'

'We have Prometheus on our wall,' said Flavia.

'He is having his liver pecked out by a bird,' added Nubia.

Lupus raised his head with interest from the feather bed.

'Jonathan,' whispered Flavia, coming closer. 'You said we might get to meet your mother if we came to Rome. When can we see her?'

'Soon, I hope,' said Jonathan, lowering his voice, too. 'Uncle Simeon will know where she is. If he's here in

Rome. It's probably too late to go to the Golden House today,' he said. 'But maybe we can go tomorrow.'

'Your uncle is not in Rome this week,' said a gruff, well-educated voice from the doorway.

They all turned to see a tall, grey-haired man with a large nose and bushy eyebrows.

'Agathus!' exclaimed Jonathan.

Agathus inclined his head. 'Welcome back to the Imperial Palace, Jonathan ben Mordecai,' he said with a smile. 'I hope your quarters are more acceptable this time?'

Jonathan grinned and said to his friends, 'The last time I visited the Emperor I ended up scrubbing latrines in the Golden House. Agathus was kind to me.' He turned back to Agathus. 'Did I ever thank you?'

'No need,' said Agathus. 'Especially to a fellow Jew. Tell me,' he glanced across the courtyard, 'have they taken your father to the island?'

'I'm not sure. I think he's gone to meet some other doctors.'

'Then he is at the sanctuary,' said Agathus. 'The Emperor has set up a clinic there to find the best treatment for the pestilence. Your father won't be back for an hour or two.'

Jonathan's heart was pounding again. 'Agathus,' he whispered. 'Do you know where my mother is?'

'Of course,' said the old steward. 'She is here on the Palatine. And she has just invited the four of you to dine in her quarters.'

SCROLL VII

As Agathus led the way through a maze of columned corridors, Nubia stared in wonder. The walls of the Imperial Palace were inlaid with panels of coloured marble – red, yellow, grey, pink, buttermilk and green. The floor was blue-grey marble, so highly polished that it looked wet. Above them a high vault was painted with panels matching the colours of the marble. The tops and bases of the columns they passed were gilded, and details on the wooden doors were also picked out in gold.

Nubia and her three friends followed Agathus up several flights of stairs, occasionally passing slaves wearing black tunics, scribes in grey or watchful guards in red tunics and gleaming armour. Presently they reached another long corridor with wine-coloured columns running before a white and cream marbled wall.

At the end of this corridor were double doors of oak, carved with cupids and doves. There were no soldiers standing at these doors.

Agathus scratched the door softly with his finger-nails, then pulled open the right-hand door and stood back. 'I will take my leave of you here,' he said, and gave a little bow.

Nubia followed Jonathan and the others through the doorway. She found herself in a room with coloured mosaic floors and blue silk divans against red-painted walls. The violet chinks of evening sky gleaming through the sandalwood window-screens showed her that they must be on one of the upper floors of the palace. A large standing loom stood in the centre of the room and near it coals glowed red in a copper brazier. As Nubia looked at the brazier, a woman dressed in a long tunic of midnight blue stepped out from behind the loom.

She was breathtakingly beautiful, thought Nubia, just like Miriam. She had the same wide-spaced eyes and full mouth, the same flawless complexion, the same exquisite curve of cheekbone and chin. But where Miriam's hair was curly, this woman's hair was as smooth as black silk.

'Mother!' cried Jonathan, and ran to her.

'Jonathan, my son,' said his mother in Hebrew. She took a step back to look at him. 'You look well: I'm glad to see you've put on weight. You were far too thin before.'

She put her hand up to his cheek and although her fingers were cool and smooth, he felt the callous of the weaver's shuttle. Up close he could see a few threads of silver in her hair and fine lines around her eyes and mouth.

She had spoken in Hebrew but he replied in Latin: 'Mother, these are my friends, the ones I've told you about, the ones who helped save your life.' He turned to his friends. 'This is my mother, Susannah.'

She looked at them with a grave smile.

'You should be Flavia. I am most glad to meet you. Most glad that you and my son are friends.'

Jonathan winced. When his mother spoke in Latin she seemed different. Less confident and less intelligent. He didn't want his friends to think she was stupid.

'This is Nubia,' he said quickly. 'And Lupus.'

'I am so happy that you come to Rome,' she said. 'But I ask you all one thing. Please do not tell Jonathan's father that I live. The . . . shame is too great.'

They nodded and Flavia said, 'We promise we won't breathe a word.'

As his mother turned back to him, Jonathan caught a whiff of her perfume: rose and myrtle.

'I'm sorry, Jonathan,' she said in Hebrew, 'you know I'm glad to see you, of course, but I wish Titus hadn't sent for your father. It's not as if he hasn't brought in dozens of the best physicians in the Roman Empire.'

'But father's one of the best, too,' he replied in Hebrew, and then in Latin, 'I had the fever recently. Father saved my life. And he saved Flavia and Lupus and almost everybody else he treated.'

'Yes,' she said. 'He was good man.'

'He still is,' said Jonathan sharply. 'He's not dead, mother.'

'Yes. I know this. But I do not understand why Titus takes . . . the risk . . . to invite him here.'

'He's worried about the prophecy,' said a soft voice. A dark-haired young woman stepped out from the shadows behind the loom.

Jonathan glanced at her, and could not stop his jaw from dropping.

Five Hebrew letters were branded across her lovely forehead. They spelled out a name: Delilah.

'Great Jupiter's eyebrows!' Flavia exclaimed. 'You've been branded!' The words were out before she could stop them and she clapped her hand to her mouth. 'I'm sorry,' she said. 'I didn't mean to . . .'

'I do not mind,' said the young woman. Her black tunic and bare feet showed that she was an imperial slave. 'Shalom.' She bowed respectfully. 'Peace be with you.'

'Delilah is my servant,' said Susannah, catching the girl's hand and giving it a squeeze. 'The Emperor's consort Berenice accused her of flirting with him a few years ago. She branded her forehead as punishment.'

'How awful!' said Flavia. Delilah was looking at them with large brown eyes and it occurred to Flavia that she would have been extremely pretty had it not been for the brand on her forehead.

'You were telling them about the prophecy,' the slave-girl prompted Susannah.

'Yes.' Jonathan's mother turned back to them. 'Titus has had what he believes is a prophetic warning: "When a Prometheus opens a Pandora's box, Rome will be devastated." '

'Pandora's box with diseases and death in it?' Nubia asked Flavia in a whisper. 'Didn't Pandora already open it?'

'It's an expression,' Flavia told her. 'We say someone has opened "a Pandora's box" when they do something that starts a chain of bad events.'

41

Jonathan frowned. 'So what does the prophecy mean?'

'Titus believes it is warning,' said Susannah in her stilted Latin. 'But he knows not what it means.'

Suddenly Flavia snapped her fingers. 'That must be the mystery the Emperor wants us to solve!' she cried. 'That's why he gave us the Prometheus room: the prophecy is the mystery!'

'It is indeed,' said the Emperor Titus, stepping into the room. 'It is indeed.'

SCROLL VIII

Titus Flavius Vespasianus was a stocky ex-soldier of about forty. He had a pleasant, square face and intelligent hazel eyes. Despite his thinning hair, his bull neck and the beginnings of a paunch, he was still handsome. But if Lupus hadn't already known he was the Emperor, he would never have guessed it.

On this cold February day, Titus was wearing two tunics and fur-lined leather slippers. The only clues to his imperial status were the many gold rings on his fingers and a short purple house-cloak.

'Greetings, Jonathan.' Leaving the door open behind him, Titus moved straight to Jonathan and lifted the sleeve of his tunic. 'How is it healing?'

'Greetings, Caesar.' Jonathan bowed his head. He had been branded five months earlier, and although the Emperor had since apologised, Lupus knew a brand could not be taken back. Jonathan would bear Titus's mark for life.

'The scar is beginning to form,' said the Emperor after a moment, 'but it still looks painful.'

'It's not too bad, Caesar,' said Jonathan. Lupus knew he was lying.

'Brave boy,' said Titus, and turned to Lupus and the girls. 'I'm glad to see you brought your keen mind with you, Flavia Gemina. But why are you all standing?' He clapped his hands and called towards the open doorway: 'Biztha! Bigtha! Bring us some hot spiced wine! And light the lamps in here.'

Titus turned back to Susannah and took her hand.

Lupus saw Jonathan clench his fists.

'Come. Sit.' Still holding Susannah's hand, Titus led them towards the silk-covered divan built against two of the room's walls. As the others followed him, Delilah brought forward a chair for the Emperor to sit on. Then she discreetly closed the open double doors and stepped back into the shadows behind Susannah's loom. Lupus and the others sat on the divan.

'I want to thank you all for coming to Rome,' said Titus. 'I haven't seen your father yet, Jonathan, because I wanted him to meet the other doctors on the Tiber Island as soon as possible. I have a serious problem.' He leaned back in his chair and the leather creaked.

'The fever here in Rome has reached epidemic proportions. Until now I have been unwilling to call it "plague" but now I fear I must. Last week, the death toll in Rome reached two thousand. I am making daily offerings at the Temples of Apollo and Aesculapius. I have summoned doctors from all over the Empire. I have also consulted my astrologer and my advisers. I wanted to know if perhaps the gods were offended by some broken vow or crime.' He looked round at them all and in the fading light his eyes looked dark.

'Then I remembered a dream I had on the Kalends of January, six weeks ago. In this dream, the god Jupiter appeared to me and spoke these words, "When a

44

Prometheus opens a Pandora's box, Rome will be devastated." '

'The plague!' cried Flavia.

Titus nodded and the chair creaked as he shifted in it. 'Some sort of Pandora's box has been opened. And this pestilence threatens to devastate Rome. I believe that if we can close the box or find this "Prometheus" – the one who opened it – then the plague will end. Until now I have only told Susannah and my astrologer Ascletario about this dream because I'm afraid—'

The double doors swung open and Titus stopped talking as two long-haired slave-boys came in; one had black hair, the other brown.

The black-haired boy began to light the lamps while the second carried in a succession of small tables and grouped them in front of the divan. On the tables were silver platters with hard-boiled quails' eggs, tiny sausages rolled in bay leaves and cubes of melon soaked in honey and garum: the first course of a light dinner.

Now Black-hair was washing their hands, pouring warm rose-scented water from a silver jug and catching the overflow in a bowl. As Lupus dried his hands on the linen napkin draped over the boy's arm, he looked up to study the slave. Black-hair was almost pretty, with upward slanting black eyes and saffron-perfumed hair as silky as Susannah's. Lupus guessed the boy was about Jonathan's age.

Jonathan was looking at his mother and didn't notice Black-hair shoot him a defiant glare, but Lupus saw it and turned to watch the boys pad out of the room on silent bare feet.

After the double doors closed behind them, Titus continued.

'Last week, I received a letter telling me of Mordecai's success in treating fever victims in Ostia. I suddenly remembered how much he helped the victims of the eruption last August, and how the four of you saved my life the following month.'

He looked round at them all, and now that the lamps had been lit, his hazel eyes gleamed green-gold. 'Not only are you clever, resourceful and brave—' here he raised his eyebrows at Lupus '—but because you are children, you can go where many adults can't. Like slaves, people do not always notice you.'

He fumbled in a hidden pocket of his wide leather belt and removed four small ivory rectangles on cords of purple silk. 'But if anyone *does* notice you, and if they challenge you, then these imperial passes will give you access to all areas. They also show that you are under my protection.'

Titus handed out the four passes. 'I will ask my astrologer to help you begin your investigation tomorrow. Ascletario is the only other person who knows of my dream – apart from those of us in this room. He also knows this city better than I do. Ascletario will direct you – personally escort you, if necessary – to any place in Rome. And these passes will grant you access.'

Titus summoned Delilah with a gesture and as she poured out seven beakers of mulsum, Lupus examined his imperial pass with interest. It was about the size of his thumb but rectangular and flat. Raised letters had been carved onto the ivory wafer and then painted red: IMP. LICET: 'the Emperor permits'. A neat hole had been bored into one end and a purple silk cord threaded through, so that the pass could be worn round the neck.

The Emperor and the others were lifting their cups so Lupus quickly slipped the cord over his head and lifted his drink as well.

'Recruiting you may be foolishness,' said the Emperor Titus, 'but I am trying every imaginable means to save my city and my people. You four may be my best hope of finding this Prometheus – whoever he may be – and of stopping the pestilence. The fate of Rome may be in your hands. I drink to you: Jonathan, Flavia, Nubia and Lupus. And to the success of your mission!'

'Isn't it exciting?' Flavia whispered to the others. 'The Emperor wants us to solve a mystery and save Rome!'

They were back in their garden suite. Slaves were warming the boys' beds with heated rods of bronze so they had all gathered in the girls' bedroom for a private conference. The four friends were sitting cross-legged on Flavia's bed, which had already been warmed.

Jonathan snorted. 'I don't believe in pagan prophecies. Even if it's true, prophecies are as slippery as oiled weasels. They can mean almost anything. Remember the prophecy that Persian king received just before he set out to conquer Greece? "If you cross a certain river you will destroy a great kingdom"?'

'It was Xerxes,' whispered Flavia. 'He crossed the river and he *did* destroy a great kingdom – his own!'

Lupus uttered a bark of laughter, and Nubia giggled.

47

Flavia nodded thoughtfully. 'You're absolutely right, Jonathan. Prophecies are never what you expect.'

'Then how are we supposed to solve this stupid mystery?' said Jonathan. 'Prometheus could be anybody.'

'Well, we could start by learning more about the real Prometheus. I mean the *mythical* Prometheus. Will you help us, Jonathan? Or do you just want to spend your time here visiting your mother?'

He was looking at the Prometheus fresco again. Flavia saw him shudder.

'Jonathan, are you all right?'

'I'm fine. It's just that . . . my brand hurts.' He turned to her. 'And who says Prometheus is bad, anyway? He only wanted to help mankind and he gets punished with eternal torment. Maybe it's Jupiter who is the bad one.'

'Jonathan!' Flavia gasped. 'You shouldn't say such a thing.'

'It's just not fair that Prometheus was punished for trying to help mankind.'

'But you'll help us, won't you? I mean, with the investigation? Even though it's only a stupid pagan prophecy?'

Jonathan grinned in spite of himself.

'Good!' said Flavia. 'Now, I wonder if there's a library on this hill?'

SCROLL IX

Flavia and her friends stood on the steps of a huge white-columned temple. They had breakfasted in their rooms and their new guide had led them out through the cold shadows to the Temple of Apollo, only a few paces from their courtyard. It gleamed in the bright morning sunshine.

'Great Neptune's beard!' Flavia tipped her head back. 'Look at the columns!'

'The white marble columns are fifty feet tall,' said Ascletario. The Emperor's astrologer was a tall, thin Egyptian with a face as brown as nutmeg and as narrow as an axe. 'Please to note the Corinthian capitals on top of them. Now, please to look inside the cella. That is the cult statue of Apollo with his sister Diana and his mother Leto. The god has set down his bow and arrows of pestilence, and taken up his lyre.'

'What's that gold box at their feet?' asked Flavia.

'That is where the books of prophecy are now kept,' said their guide.

Lupus tugged Flavia's tunic and pointed behind them.

Jonathan turned, too, and gave a low whistle. 'Look at that view!' They turned their backs on the statues and looked out through the columns.

'This is the Circus Maximus directly below us,' said Ascletario. He turned to the right. 'And through those columns is the Roman forum.'

'What is that pink temple?' asked Nubia, pointing to a temple on top of the hill behind the forum.

'That temple is nothing less than the symbol of Rome,' said Ascletario, rubbing his hands like a fly. 'It is the Temple of Jupiter Optimus Maximus. Best and greatest. Greatest and best.'

They looked at him.

'Best and greatest.'

'Why is it pink?' asked Flavia. 'And it looks a bit squashed.'

'Please to note that the white columns are painted with red stripes,' said Ascletario, 'in the Etruscan fashion. From a distance they give the impression of pinkness. Do you see the pediment? The triangular part on top of the columns? Please to note it is open, with no scene depicted inside. And the lower, broader proportions of the whole temple are also Etruscan, Etruscan, Etruscan.'

'So that hill is the Capitoline!' cried Flavia. 'Where the famous geese live!'

Ascletario bobbed his head.

'Geese?' Nubia looked up with interest.

'That hill was the first citadel of Rome,' explained Flavia. 'And once when the barbarians were creeping up it to attack, some geese raised the alarm and saved the city! So now they are sacred geese and nobody can hurt them.'

Ascletario nodded again.

'And where's the Tarpeian Rock?' asked Flavia. 'It's also on the Capitoline, isn't it?'

'It is,' said Ascletario. 'That cliff to the left of the temple – nearest the river – is the Tarpeian Rock.'

'What is tar pee un rock?'

'It's a cliff with razor-sharp rocks at the bottom,' said Flavia. 'They throw traitors off it.'

This time it was Lupus who looked up with interest.

Ascletario gave a small bow and said to Flavia, 'You are very knowledgeable. I think you will like what I am about to show you. Please to come with me.'

One side of the Temple of Apollo almost touched the Imperial Palace. Ascletario led them around to the back of the temple and down some steps. On either side stretched two beautiful colonnades with red tile roofs and yellow columns. Between the columns were statues of alternating red marble and black marble.

'Behold!' whispered Nubia. 'What is happening to the poor statue people?'

Flavia saw that the black statues were of boys and the red ones of girls, and that all of them were shown writhing in agony.

Lupus mimed someone being shot by an arrow in the neck.

'He's right!' cried Jonathan. 'Some of the statues have bronze arrows in them. No, all of them.'

'They're Niobe's children!' cried Flavia and looked at Ascletario.

'Correct.' He gave a little bow.

'Who are my oh bees?' asked Nubia.

'Ny-oh-bee. She had fourteen children, seven boys

and seven girls. She boasted that she had more children than the goddess Leto, who only had two.'

'Uh-oh,' said Jonathan.

And Lupus scribbled a word on his wax tablet:

HUBRIS!

'Exactly,' said Flavia grimly. 'It just so happened that Leto's two children were Apollo and Diana. They killed all Niobe's fourteen children to punish her for her hubris.'

'Please to note,' said Ascletario, 'that Apollo is the god of plague and his arrows strike men down.'

Suddenly Flavia noticed that the inner wall of the colonnade was covered with niches and shelves.

'Great Neptune's Jupiter!' she gasped. 'It's a library. I've never seen so many scrolls!'

Ascletario bowed. 'It is one of the finest libraries in the Roman Empire. On the right you have the Greek. On the left the Latin. The Latin . . .' he gestured with his left hand '. . . and the Greek.' He gestured with his right. 'The Greek and the Latin. The Latin and the Greek.'

Behind him Lupus was imitating his hand gestures and Flavia turned quickly so the guide wouldn't see her laugh.

'Are there any scrolls by Aeschylus here?' she asked, when she had regained her composure.

'Of course, of course, of course. Do you want your Aeschylus in the original Greek?' he asked, rubbing his hands together. 'Or in translation?'

Flavia considered for a moment. 'May I have one of

each?' she asked. 'My Greek isn't good enough for me to read it on its own. But if I have the translation beside it . . .'

'Certainly, certainly, certainly,' said Ascletario. He led them between a black marble boy and a yellow column into the Latin section of the colonnade. It was flooded with pure morning light except where the columns cast their shadows. 'Take a seat at this table and I'll be back in a moment.' He turned to go, then swivelled in a full circle as Flavia cried:

'Wait! Can you bring Apollodorus, too? And Hesiod in translation?'

Ascletario bowed and trotted off towards the Greek colonnade.

They sat at the marble table and looked up and down the long room. A moment later Flavia felt Jonathan's elbow in her ribs.

'Josephus!' he hissed.

'What?'

'The man writing at that table over there – the man with the beard – I'm sure that's Josephus.'

'The man who exposed you and your uncle when you tried to sneak into the palace in disguise?' asked Flavia.

Jonathan nodded.

They all stared at the bearded man. Suddenly he glanced up so all four of them dropped their heads, pretending to study the coloured swirls in the marble table top.

A moment later his shadow fell across the table as he stood between them and the columns.

SCROLL X

Flavia studied the bearded man who was smiling down at Jonathan. She guessed he was about the same age as Mordecai: in his early forties.

'You're Jonathan, aren't you?' he said. 'Simeon's nephew. We met a few months ago.'

'I remember,' said Jonathan coldly.

'I am sorry.' The man spoke with an accent like Mordecai's. 'I was only acting in the best interests of the Emperor.'

'I know,' said Jonathan, and examined the table top.

The bearded man's smile faltered and he looked at Flavia and the others. 'My name is Josephus,' he said. 'I'm writing a history of the Jewish people, and the Emperor has put his library at my disposal. May I ask what you are doing here?'

'We're just doing some research for a project,' said Flavia. 'Um . . . a project on um . . . Greek tragedy.'

'Well, if I can help in any way, don't hesitate to ask.' He looked at Jonathan. 'You can find me here most days.'

'Thank you very much,' said Flavia.

'Ah,' murmured Josephus. 'Here comes Ascletario. You must excuse me. His chatter always gives me a headache.'

A moment later Ascletario triumphantly deposited three scrolls and two scroll cases on the marble table.

'Was that man bothering you?' he said, narrowing his eyes at Josephus's retreating back.

'Not at all,' said Flavia brightly and looked through the scrolls. 'Excellent,' she said. 'We have Aeschylus, Apollodorus and Hesiod. In both Greek and Latin. Thank you, Ascletario.'

'I humbly bow.'

Flavia glanced up at their guide, still hovering. She wasn't ready to trust him.

'Ascletario,' she said sweetly, 'could you please find us some pictures of Prometheus? Maybe on some vases?'

'Certainly, certainly, certainly,' he bobbed his narrow head. 'Please to note the Emperor has a fine collection of Greek pottery. I will return shortly.'

As soon as he was out of sight, Flavia turned to the others. 'In order to discover who is the Prometheus in Titus's dream, we need to find out what the mythical Prometheus was like. His character. For example, Nubia is gentle and good with animals. And Lupus is quick-tempered. I mean brave!' she said hastily, as Lupus narrowed his eyes at her. 'Very brave!' She grinned. 'So look for the qualities that make Prometheus special.'

Jonathan stared at the black letters on the papyrus scroll of Hesiod.

But he did not see the words.

He was imagining how it might happen.

His mother would be walking down one corridor of the palace and his father down another. Suddenly they would turn a corner, come face to face and instantly recognise one another. His father would be overcome by his mother's beauty and would forgive her there and then. And she – finally free of her guilt – would beg him to take her back. They would go to Titus hand in hand, and the Emperor's heart would be softened by their love and he would give Susannah his permission to leave.

Then things would be right in the world. They would all return to Ostia where his father would cure people and his mother would cook and weave wool and sing in a voice half-remembered from so long ago. And they would be a family again.

A tear splashed onto the papyrus and one of the words blurred as the ink dissolved: the word 'chaos'. Jonathan hastily blotted it with the long sleeve of his winter tunic and glanced round guiltily, relieved to see no one had noticed his defacement of a priceless scroll.

'Interesting,' murmured Flavia. She looked up at her three friends. 'Has anybody found any clues?'

'I feel sick from the smoke,' said Nubia quietly.

'What? Oh, the incense in that brazier is to purify the air. So we don't catch the plague. Did you find anything?'

'Yes,' said Nubia. She had been reading the easiest text: Apollodorus translated into Latin. 'I find that Prometheus he brings fire in a stalk of fennel. Like the fennel Alma puts in stew.'

'That's right,' said Flavia. 'Anything else?'

'Yes,' said Nubia slowly. 'You said Prometheus is

56

being tied or chained, but I think this word means "nailed". He is nailed to a mountain.'

Flavia leaned over to look. 'You're right, Nubia. That word means nailed.'

'Like men on the road to Rome,' said Nubia.

'Crucified,' murmured Jonathan. 'Prometheus suffers eternal torment.'

'How about you, Lupus?' said Flavia. 'I've just reached the lines in the play where Prometheus says he gave mankind medicine and prophecy. Have you got to that part?'

Lupus shook his head, pointed at the scroll and gave an exaggerated shrug.

'Is the Greek too difficult for you?'

Lupus swivelled his open hand at the wrist, as if to say: A bit.

'Did you find anything, Jonathan?'

Jonathan shook his head.

'Well, I did,' said Flavia. 'Listen to this: "There was no help for man, no healing food, unguent, or potion, until I showed him how to mix mild medicines which fight all sorts of sickness." '

Flavia looked round at them, her eyes gleaming with excitement. 'Don't you see? Prometheus was the first doctor. I'll bet a million sestercii that our "Prometheus" is a doctor. Maybe even one of the doctors with your father, Jonathan. I think that's where we should begin our investigations.'

'Behold!' cried Nubia. 'Boat with trees and temples on it. It is the biggest boat I have ever seen.'

Ascletario shook his narrow head. He had led them down the Palatine Hill, past the Forum Boarium and through the River Gate of the town walls. Now they were walking beside the river, with the milky green water flowing on their left and the stalls of the medicine market on their right.

'No, no, no, Miss Nubia. It is not a boat,' said Ascletario. 'It is the Tiber Island.'

'The Tiger Island?' Nubia's heart stuttered.

'No, no, no. The Tiber Island. The Tiber is the name of this river: Tiber, Tiber, Tiber. It is not a ship. No. It is a small island. It was already boat-shaped so they built a giant prow on the front, a stern at the back, curved sides between. Then they erected that obelisk – seventy feet tall – to give the appearance of a mast. Now the island resembles a ship, a ship, a ship.'

They stared at him.

'A ship,' said Ascletario.

'Why does it resemble to a ship?' Nubia looked towards the red-roofed temples among poplars and plane trees on the boat-shaped island.

'Three hundred and seventy years ago there was a terrible plague in Rome. The first plague ever. They tried to discover its cure, or at least its cause. And so they consulted the Sibylline books—'

'The what books?' asked Jonathan.

'The Sibylline, Sibylline, Sibylline . . . The Sibyl is the priestess who lives in Cumae near the Bay of Neapolis.'

'Remember when we read Virgil's *Aeneid* to Nubia last summer?' cried Flavia. 'The Sibyl was the priestess who guided Aeneas to the underworld.'

'I remember!' said Nubia with excitement. 'She gives Cerberus a sleepy honeycake.'

'Correct,' said Ascletario. 'This same Sibyl foretold everything that would happen to Rome in the future, and she wrote it down in scrolls. Those are the Sibylline books. They told the city fathers how to cure the plague.'

'Then why don't they consult them now?' asked Jonathan.

'The Sibylline books were kept in a stone chest underneath the Temple of Jupiter on the Capitoline Hill. Right up there!' Ascletario turned and pointed at the temple visible above the city wall on their right.

'The pink temple again!' said Nubia, shading her eyes. 'I see the stripes now. It is very charming with the blue sky behind.'

'Although it looks old, that temple is new,' said Ascletario. 'Please to note it was rebuilt to look exactly like its Etruscan predecessor. The Sibylline books were destroyed when the temple burned down the first time. The Emperor Augustus tried to reconstruct them.' Ascletario heaved a deep sigh. 'Please to note they are now no longer useful. Do you remember the gold box at the foot of Apollo in the Temple on the Palatine Hill?'

They nodded.

'That is where the new books are kept.'

Nubia glanced at Flavia. She knew they were both thinking the same thing.

'Has that box been opened recently?' asked Flavia.

'It is opened daily,' sighed Ascletario. 'Please to note

the priests are scouring the books for some wisdom about this pestilence. But there is nothing in them. The original books would have told us what to do . . .' he sighed again.

Flavia turned to Ascletario. 'Could the old books *really* tell the future?'

He nodded. 'The Sibylline books said that the first plague would end when Aesculapius came from Greece to Rome.'

'What is eye school ape pee us?' asked Nubia.

'Aesculapius is the god of healing. Beg pardon.' The crowd before them had parted and their Egyptian guide extended his arms protectively as a cart full of dead bodies passed by. Around them, men and women were making the sign against evil. Nubia did so as well.

'The story of how Aesculapius came to Rome is told by Ovid,' continued their guide, when the cart had passed by.

'Pater won't let me read Ovid,' said Flavia. 'He keeps it on the top shelf behind the Catullus. But I do know that Aesculapius was the son of Apollo. And that he became such a good doctor that one day he brought a man back from the dead!'

Ascletario nodded. 'Please to note that the gods could not allow a mere mortal to perform such a godlike act.'

Lupus flicked open his wax tablet to the word he had written earlier:

HUBRIS

'Correct,' said their guide, 'and so Jupiter killed Aesculapius with a thunderbolt.'

'Jupiter and his thunderbolts again,' muttered Jonathan. 'Blasting another person who just wanted to help.'

'Poor Aesculapius,' said Nubia.

'He became a god of the underworld. And so did his pet snake.'

'Of all creatures, I do not like the snake,' Nubia said in a small voice.

'Not to worry,' said Ascletario. 'The snake is benevolent, benevolent, benevolent.'

'That's right, Nubia,' said Flavia with a smile. 'Everybody knows snakes bring good luck and protection.'

'And healing,' said Ascletario. 'When the wise men of Rome went to the sanctuary of Aesculapius in Epidauros, they brought back the god in the form of a snake. As the returning boat sailed into Rome, it passed this island, and the snake slithered off the boat and swam ashore. That very hour the plague stopped. In gratitude, the Romans built a temple to Aesculapius and placed his statue inside. They even made the island look like the boat, so that the snake would feel at home. Here we are.' He paused and gestured to the island, whose bridge they were just about to cross. 'This is Snake Island, where Romans come if they are too poor to afford a doctor.'

Nubia looked at him. 'We are going to Snake Island?'

'Correct.'

Nubia shuddered. The feeling of dread had returned.

SCROLL XI

Now that he was a ship-owner, Lupus knew the front of a ship was called the prow and the back the stern. The road which crossed over the bridge divided the boat-shaped Tiber Island into two sections: the prow was about a third the length of the island and the stern the remaining two thirds. The obelisk, trees and biggest temple were at the prow, which pointed downstream, towards Ostia.

'Stay close, watch out for pickpockets,' warned Ascletario, as they were jostled across the bridge by the crowds funnelling onto the island.

Presently Lupus found himself standing in a crowded space near the obelisk. Up above, big seagulls wheeled silently in the clear blue sky.

'On your left is the Temple of Aesculapius,' said their guide. 'Please to note that people with incurable diseases bathe in the water from the well and sleep near the sacred grove, in a precinct called the abaton. They hope that the god will visit them in their dreams and cure them. And here on your right is the Temple of Jupiter.'

Lupus frowned, tugged Ascletario's long tunic and pointed back towards the pink temple on the Capitoline above the city wall.

'What? Oh, you want to know why there is a temple to Jupiter down here as well as up there?'

Lupus nodded.

'There are many temples to Jupiter here in Rome. That is because Jupiter has many aspects. Behind *this* Temple of Jupiter are more porticoes for the sick who cannot afford doctors. That is where the Emperor has set up a clinic. You find your doctors there. Priests in the sanctuary,' he gestured with one hand, 'doctors in the clinic,' he gestured with the other. 'Priests, sanctuary; doctors, clinic. The sanctuary, the clinic.'

Lupus's head was beginning to throb when he heard the faint sound of music.

'Hark!' said Nubia. 'I am hearing flutes and drums.'

Lupus pointed back towards the bridge they had just crossed. He jumped up a few times, trying to see between the people crowding the square.

'Behold!' said Nubia, as the crowd parted. 'Men leading a bull. And the Titus is among them.'

'He's going to sacrifice it, isn't he,' asked Flavia. 'And ask Aesculapius to stop the plague.'

Ascletario rubbed his hands together and bobbed his head. 'Yes. Please to note Titus has sacrificed a bull here every day for the past week.'

Lupus wanted to see the bull sacrificed, so he tugged Flavia's tunic and pointed hopefully towards the temple.

'Are we allowed to watch?' asked Flavia.

'We are not allowed in the sanctuary but we can look over the wall here. Follow me, follow me, follow me.'

★

Nubia liked the honey-coloured, red-roofed Temple of Aesculapius. It stood against a backdrop of green poplars, chestnuts and plane trees. Among the trees and around the temple were dozens of statues and markers, dedicated by those who had been healed, according to Ascletario.

In front of the temple – near the slender obelisk – was the altar, a long block of creamy yellow marble the same colour as the temple, carved and painted with scenes from the life of Aesculapius. On top of the altar Nubia could see offerings of honeycakes and gar-lands.

To her left, musicians led the procession through the sanctuary gate. Nubia watched the flautist with particular interest; he played an aulos, or double flute. She liked the buzzing sound it made and one day she hoped to own one. Behind the musicians came the priest, his assistants, a pretty black bull with gilded horns, and finally the Emperor.

'Behold!' said Nubia. 'Why does the bull wear a crown of flowers, like a bride?'

'The garland shows the animal is perfect, perfect, perfect,' said Ascletario.

'He dies because he is perfect?'

'That is correct. You must give a perfect offering to the gods.'

'Why is the Titus now also putting on a crown of leaves? Is he perfect, too?'

'The Emperor has recently accepted the office of Chief Priest. He is going to perform the sacrifice. Please to note the garland separates one thing from all the others. Titus's garland shows that he is set apart, chosen, holy.'

'I've never seen a priest wear a garland before,' said Flavia.

'You are correct. It is unusual for a Roman to wear the crown while sacrificing. This is the Greek way. But Coronis – the mother of Aesculapius – appeared to one of the Emperor's advisors in a dream.'

'Coronis!' cried Flavia. 'Her name means "garland".'

'Correct. In this dream Coronis warned Agathus that unless Titus wore a garland whenever he acted as priest, then the plague would not end.'

'Agathus?' said Jonathan sharply.

'Another dream!' exclaimed Nubia.

Ascletario nodded and pointed. 'Now Titus covers his head with his toga so that he will not accidentally see or hear anything of ill omen. That is why the musicians play that shrill air, to cover any unhappy groan the bull might make. The victim should go willingly to the sacrifice or the god will not accept it.'

'They drug the bull, don't they?' asked Jonathan.

'Yes,' said Ascletario. 'The bull's last meal was fine grain with herbs that make him tranquil and stop him feeling pain. And there! Did you see how deftly the priest's helper strikes the back of the bull's head? So that the creature sinks gently to his knees? He is dazed and now Titus can cut his throat.'

As the blood spurted out, Nubia turned her head away. She hated to see any animal die, especially a beautiful bull like this one, with his crown of sweet-smelling flowers slipping down over his rolling brown eyes.

'Now the priest will cut open the bull and examine his inner organs. After that they will butcher him. The good parts of his meat will be roasted and fed to the sick here in the sanctuary. Usually it goes to the priests, but they have more than enough this week.'

'I know what happens next,' said Flavia. 'They wrap up the gristle and bone in fat and burn it on the altar. Just like Prometheus taught them to do. And that's another reason Jupiter was angry with Prometheus; he tricked the gods into thinking they were getting the best part.'

'Shhh!' hissed Ascletario. He looked around nervously. 'Do not say such a thing. The Temple of Jupiter is just behind us and the god may hear you.' And in an unnaturally loud voice he announced, 'The gods love the fragrant smell of burning fat. It is a sweet savour to their nostrils, their nostrils, their nostrils.'

'It's over now, Nubia,' said Jonathan. 'You can look.'

'It is time for me to return to the palace,' said Ascletario. 'Shall I come back for you later?'

'I think we can find our way back to the palace,' said Flavia. 'Thank you very much for your help.'

'I humbly bow.' He backed away for a few steps, bobbing his head and rubbing his hands together like a fly. Then he turned and disappeared into the crowd.

'Let's go to the clinic, where the doctors are,' said Flavia, 'and see if we can find our Prometheus.'

Jonathan pulled a long face. 'The clinic, the sanctuary. Clinic, sanctuary. Sanctuary, clinic!'

Flavia laughed.

But Nubia did not laugh. She did not smell any sweet

savour. She only smelled blood. Suddenly she looked around.

'Lupus!' she cried. 'Where is the Lupus?'

SCROLL XII

Lupus stepped into the innermost room of the temple, a narrow cella with small high windows. It was late morning and beams of pale sunlight sliced down through the incense-smoky gloom. One fat sunbeam illuminated the cult statue. The god Aesculapius was shown with curly hair and beard, wearing something like a toga and leaning on a staff round which a large snake coiled. The statue was painted and the down-ward slanting light threw the god's eyes into shadow. It seemed as if Aesculapius really stood there, looking straight down at him.

Lupus shivered and glanced around. He was alone.

He reached into his belt pouch and pulled out a small object. Was it wrong to dedicate something stolen to the god? He hoped not. He hadn't stolen it because he had no money. He had stolen it because he didn't want the others to know.

Feeling slightly dizzy from the incense, he stepped towards the Healer, the son of Apollo.

He took one more look at the object in his hand: a little tongue moulded of clay. Then he laid it at the god's feet and in his mind he prayed:

Dear Aesculapius, please heal me. Please give me back my tongue.

'Lupus! Where have you been?' said Flavia. 'If we lost you here in Rome we'd never find you again! It was bad enough that time—'

Flavia swallowed the rest of her words and cursed silently. That was not the way to deal with Lupus. An open rebuke usually made him angry. She braced herself for a rude gesture or a hasty exit, and was amazed when he dropped his head and held up his hands – palms out – as if to say: You're right. I'm sorry.

'It's just . . . we were worried about you,' she said, and was surprised to find tears springing to her eyes. She turned away quickly, before Lupus could see. 'Let's see if these imperial passes work,' she said briskly.

There was a long queue of people waiting at a gate beside the Temple of Jupiter. Some carried family members on pallets and others held sick children in their arms. One man pushed a wheelbarrow. At first glance it seemed to be full of rags, but when Flavia looked again she saw an old woman's face glaring out at her. Some of the fever victims were able to stand, but they were coughing up phlegm and spitting blood.

'I'm sorry,' a temple attendant was telling the people. 'There is no more room in the sanctuary. Try again tomorrow. There should be places then.' He nodded towards a priest pushing an empty body-cart.

Flavia held the ivory plaque in front of her and tried to catch his eye.

'But where can I take my daughter?' cried a man in a patched brown tunic. He held a little girl of about five in his arms. 'We can't afford the doctor.'

'Take your sick to the gardens across the river,' said a commanding voice that Flavia recognised as the Emperor's. 'I have made provision for many to be treated there as well as here. You will find food and water and someone to nurse your loved ones.'

The crowd parted and Titus appeared.

'Caesar is great! Caesar is merciful!' sobbed an old man, falling at Titus's feet and pressing his lips fervently to the imperial boot.

Titus allowed the old man to worship him for a moment. Presently he lifted him to his feet, murmured a few words, and dismissed him with a pat on the shoulder.

Flavia was close enough to hear Titus say to one of the guards in a low voice, 'Give each of these people a silver coin. But discreetly. We don't want a riot. And let that little girl and her father in.' At that moment he caught sight of Flavia and her friends. His face lit up.

'Children!' he cried. '*Salvete!* Have your investigations brought you here?'

'Yes, Caesar!' said Flavia. 'We think "Prometheus" may be one of the doctors.'

'Really?' He raised an eyebrow. 'Then you'd better come in with me. I haven't met your father yet, Jonathan, nor have I thanked him for coming. Will you introduce me to him?'

Jonathan heard the armour of the praetorian guard clinking and was aware of the Emperor close behind him as he stepped into the long portico. He glanced round quickly, trying to get his bearings and find his father.

He saw a narrow physic garden with long rows of columns stretching before him on both the right and the left: two covered walkways.

As he started to walk under cover of the right-hand colonnade, Jonathan saw that a long row of tiny rooms opened out onto it. Although the cells were narrow – barely wide enough for one bed – they were bright and well-ventilated because each looked straight out through red-based columns into the tree-filled court-yard. He glanced left and saw that the garden was filled with healing trees like laurel, myrtle, wormwood and walnut. He also noted ferns, mint, mallow, fennel, radishes and parsley. All useful for medicinal purposes.

Mingled with the cool green scent of the plants and trees was the familiar odour of the doctor's consulting room. Purifying incense rose from the braziers: frankin-cense, camphor and myrrh. Jonathan also recognised the pleasant smell of herbs crushed in marble mortars – cloves, mustard, rose, anise and hellebore – and the much less pleasant smell of human sweat, urine and burning flesh from the cauteries.

Doctors, identifiable by their aprons, moved in and out of the cells. Some worked at tables set between columns of the covered walkway. Others stood over their patients in the cells, burning flesh, letting blood or helping them to vomit.

'There's your father,' said Flavia, pointing.

In one of the cells in the colonnade across the garden a tall doctor was bending over a man on a low bed.

Jonathan shook his head in wonder. 'I still can't get used to seeing him without his turban and beard,' he murmured. And in a louder voice he said to the Emperor, 'That's my father, Caesar. Let me introduce you.'

SCROLL XIII

'Tell me, Doctor Mordecai ben Ezra,' said the Emperor after Jonathan had made the introductions, 'what do you think? Can this plague be stopped?'

Mordecai was wiping his hands on his apron. 'I would not call this a plague, Caesar, but rather an epidemic. This is a quotidian fever with chills, shivering and aching muscles. Usually in such cases the patient recovers within a few days, but with the weakest – the very old or very young – the illness goes to a more severe stage. Then the lungs become full of phlegm and the patient drowns, even though he is far from water.'

Mordecai glanced back into a cell towards one of his patients, a young man of about twenty-one.

He lowered his voice. 'But this particular fever is unlike any I have met before. What I saw in Ostia – what I see here in Rome – seems to be afflicting not only the young and the old, but also those of middle years, between fifteen and thirty-five. And in some cases it strikes with terrible swiftness. I heard of a case in Ostia last week. Four soldiers playing knucklebones together in the morning were struck down by the fever at noon and by evening three of the four men were dead.'

'Yes,' said Titus, folding his arms across his chest and

looking around. 'I have heard similar stories. Do you have any idea why this is happening?'

Jonathan held his breath. Some Jews believed God was angry with Titus for destroying the temple.

Mordecai paused. 'One possibility,' he said at last, 'is the fine ash in the air, from the eruption of Vesuvius. That ash makes people cough and weakens their lungs.'

'But the eruption was months ago!' cried Titus.

'I'm afraid its effects will be felt for a long time,' said Mordecai. 'And there is another possible link between the volcano and this epidemic. Vesuvius sent many refugees to different parts of Italia, to Ostia and Rome in particular. I believe these refugees may have brought seeds of disease with them.'

'What can be done to cure those with the fever?' asked Titus. He began walking along the row of cells and Mordecai fell into step beside him. Jonathan and his friends followed, the clinking guards took up the rear.

'They must be put to rest in a light, well-aired room.' Mordecai gestured towards one of the cells. 'These are perfect.'

'But there aren't enough of them here,' said Titus. 'I've had to open a portico in the gardens across the river.'

'Good,' said Mordecai, nodding. 'That is good. The patients should be fed broth, if they can take it, and they should drink water and wine on alternate days. Also – and this is important – they must not be bled. I believe this weakens them unnecessarily. Finally, if the fever goes to the next stage and fluid fills their lungs, they must be made to bring it up. I have discovered that if

74

patients breathe the steam from certain herbs boiled in water, it helps them cough.'

'That is your special method of treatment?' asked Titus. 'Steam promoting a cough? Nothing more?'

'Only prayer,' said Mordecai. 'As Hippocrates himself said, "The gods are the real physicians, though people do not think so."'

'Well, you seem to have had great success in Ostia. I will be interested to see how you get on today. Perhaps you and the children will join me for dinner later this afternoon in my private winter triclinium?'

Mordecai inclined his head.

'Excellent. I'll send a litter to pick you up at the tenth hour. Meanwhile, I will leave you to get on with your work.'

'OK,' whispered Flavia after Titus had gone. 'Here's our *modus operandi*. It'll be quicker if we split up and look for likely suspects.' The four friends were standing beneath a cherry tree in the medicine garden.

'We are looking for the doctor named Prometheus?' asked Nubia, pulling her lionskin cloak closer round her shoulders.

'No, Nubia,' said Flavia as patiently as she could. 'Not a doctor *named* Prometheus but someone *like* Prometheus, who was the first physician. That's why we've come here, where all the doctors are.'

'So we look for the doctor, not the patient?' asked Nubia.

'That's right,' said Flavia, keeping her voice low. 'If he's like Prometheus he'll be very clever and arrogant and think he knows best. Hubris. Remember what Aristo said about hubris?'

Nubia nodded. 'Overweening pride.'

'That may be hard,' said Jonathan.

'Why? You don't think we'll find a proud doctor?'

'Just the opposite. Father says in his experience most doctors think they're one step down from Jupiter.'

Flavia laughed. 'That's what we'll look for then. Find a doctor who thinks he's one step down from Jupiter. We'll meet back here by this cherry tree at midday to report on our findings. Oh, and keep your eyes open for any suspicious boxes.'

Nubia walked slowly along the colonnade. The name MORDICÆ had been written in chalk to the right of several of the doorways and she realised that each of the doctors had about a dozen patients under their care. All the cells marked 'Mordicae' had thin curtains made of unbleached cream-coloured linen.

Presently she was passing cells with gauzy red curtains. Some of these curtains were pulled right across, screening the occupant from view, but most were open. Nubia saw that most of the patients in these cells were asleep or unconscious. They were all very pale and some had skin so white it was almost blue. One or two were moaning, coughing into chamber-pots beside their narrow beds, but most were still as statues. They must have a graver illness than Mordecai's patients, she thought.

She noticed the doctor's name had been scrawled in charcoal to the right of each of the red-curtained doorways: DIAULUS.

Presently she came to a cell with three people in it: a worried-looking young woman sitting up in her narrow bed, the doctor seated on a folding stool, and a standing young man, probably the doctor's apprentice. The apprentice was fumbling with a bell-shaped object. Nubia recognised it at once. It was a cupping vessel like the one Lupus had shown her. She shuddered. The doctor – presumably Diaulus – was about to bleed the young woman. He was a big bald man with a smooth olive complexion.

'Bring me my wound box,' he said to his apprentice. The chinless young man set a small box on a folding table beside his master, who was still seated. Diaulus twisted his torso, examined the contents of the box and withdrew a scalpel.

As Nubia paused in the doorway to watch, Diaulus raised his head and gave her a brief glare.

'Get out of the doorway,' he said coldly. 'Out of my light.'

Nubia moved hastily out of the cell's doorway, then peeked round it just far enough to see into the room.

'Is that ready yet?' Diaulus asked his assistant.

'Yes, sir,' stammered the young apprentice. He dropped a piece of burning lint into the shiny bronze cup.

'Good,' said Diaulus, and Nubia watched in horrified fascination as he took the sharp scalpel and plunged it into the plump white crook of the woman's elbow.

SCROLL XIV

Diaulus had cut a vein in the woman's arm and as the blood began to spurt, he took the cup from his assistant and pressed it to the white flesh. The woman sat quivering and biting her lip. Presently, when the cup was full and blood began to seep over its edge, Diaulus handed it to his assistant and quickly wrapped a strip of linen around her arm.

'Empty it in the garden as usual,' he said, after briefly inspecting it.

As the assistant moved out of the cell and passed through the columns into the garden, Nubia saw Mordecai approaching.

Jonathan's father glanced at the red blood being poured away onto the ground and frowned.

'I must tell you, colleague,' he said, turning to Diaulus, 'that I am opposed to blood-letting during this pestilence. It can prove useful for hysterical women or robust people with minor complaints, but I believe it weakens those with fever.'

'Wool fluff!' Diaulus rounded on Mordecai with blazing eyes. 'Utter wool fluff! Blood-letting is a proven method. It helps almost every complaint. Don't you know that blood causes decay? Don't you know that the festering blood will poison a wound? Blood is bad.'

'Blood is not bad. Blood is good.' Mordecai spoke quietly but Nubia noticed his accent becoming more pronounced, as it did when he was upset. 'Our holy book says the life is in the blood. When you pour out blood you pour out life.'

'I don't give a speck of fluff for your holy books!' snorted Diaulus. 'You must be crazy to believe that.'

'It is not purely a Jewish belief. Some of the most respected physicians were also opposed to blood-letting. Erasistratus for example.'

'Erasistratus was an idiot,' huffed Diaulus. 'Next you'll be telling me that blood does no harm when it leaks from the veins into the arteries!'

'Sir,' said Mordecai, 'I studied medicine in Babylon and Alexandria. I have operated on living bodies and I have dissected dead ones. I believe the arteries are not filled with air – as most doctors claim – but with blood, just as the veins are.'

'Blood in the arteries?' Diaulus gave a bark of laughter and turned away in disgust. 'Now I know you're crazy,' he said.

'That smells nice,' said Flavia, as she watched the doctor massaging a patient. 'Is it myrrh and jasmine?'

The aproned doctor turned to her with a look of pleasure on his face.

'Why yes,' he said. 'You've got a good nose.'

'So do you,' said Flavia, staring. He was a young man with jet black hair, liquid brown eyes and the most enormous nose she had ever seen. 'I mean . . .'

'Don't worry!' the young doctor laughed. 'Everyone stares. I don't mind. My nose is my livelihood.'

'What do you mean?' She took a step into the cell.

'I can smell disease and I can sense the cure.' He leaned towards her, closed his eyes and sniffed. 'I can tell that you wear lemon-blossom perfume, myrtle hair-oil, and you recently soaked in a bath scented with lavender oil.'

Flavia's jaw dropped.

'For breakfast this morning you had goat's cheese and bread, washed down with well-watered spiced wine—'

'How can you—'

'Tac!' said the doctor, holding up his hand. 'Falernian wine with cinnamon, pepper and honey.' He opened his eyes and raised his eyebrows. 'Correct?'

Flavia nodded. 'That's amazing! I don't know what kind of wine it was but it did have cinnamon and honey. Pepper, too. How did you know that?'

'The proboscis,' he said, tapping his nose. 'Worth its weight.'

She laughed. 'My name's Flavia Gemina. Daughter of Marcus Flavius Geminus, sea captain.'

'Titus Flavius Cosmus,' he replied with a smile.

'Titus Flavius . . . Then you're one of the Emperor's freedmen?'

'I am.' Still smiling, he bent over his patient – a big man with a hairy back – and resumed his kneading and rubbing. 'What are you doing here?' he asked. You smell very healthy to me . . .'

'I am healthy. I'm here with my friend Jonathan.

He's the son of Doctor Mordecai. The new doctor over there across the garden.'

Cosmus glanced over his shoulder.

'The tall man talking with Diaulus? A Jew, if I'm not mistaken . . .'

Flavia nodded. 'The Emperor invited him to the clinic to help find a cure for the fever. How are *your* patients?'

'Good!' said the man on the bed in a muffled voice. He was obviously enjoying his massage.

'You hear that?' said Cosmus. 'A satisfied customer.'

The man on the bed coughed: a deep hacking cough that echoed off the walls of the small room.

'That cough doesn't sound very good,' said Flavia.

'Oh but it is! He needs to bring up the phlegm! Better out than in.'

The man obliged Cosmus by spitting into the basin beside his bed.

'That's what Doctor Mordecai says,' began Flavia doubtfully, 'but I don't know if—'

'Tac!' Cosmus held up a finger. 'Flavia Gemina, in all modesty, I am the best doctor in Rome. I follow the school of Asclepiades. Have you heard of his five principles?'

Flavia shook her head and took out her wax tablet.

'The five principles of Asclepiades are these: fasting, abstinence, walking, rocking and massage.'

'Rocking? What's that?'

'Going for a ride in a well-sprung carriage. It loosens the phlegm and the noxious humours.'

'You prescribe carriage-rides for ill people?' said Flavia.

'Of course. Not these patients, however.' Cosmus applied his elbow to a spot between the man's backbone and shoulder blade. 'For those suffering from the pestilence, I prescribe fasting during the fever and *massage*,' here he pressed with his elbow, 'after the fever. That's my maxim.'

'It's working!' said the man on the bed, and again coughed up a rich harvest of phlegm.

Cosmus rose smiling and wiped his oily hands on a towel. 'See? I am the best doctor in Rome.' He held up his index finger. 'Not the richest, mind you, but the best.'

'Thank you, best doctor in the world,' grunted Hairy-back from the bed. 'I'll sleep now.'

Flavia stepped back as Cosmus emerged from the cell.

'Sweet dreams,' said Cosmus, and pulled a gauzy blue curtain across the doorway, and then, 'Why are you looking at me like that?' he asked Flavia with twinkling eyes.

She glanced around. 'I'm not being impolite, but isn't it hubris,' she whispered, 'to say you're the best?'

He shrugged. 'It's not hubris. It's the truth. Thanks to the five principles of Asclepiades and my skilled fingers and especially my nose, I am the best!'

Flavia narrowed her eyes to give him a sceptical look.

He grinned. 'To be the best I need the biggest. Now tell me, Flavia Gemina, is this not the biggest nose you have ever seen?'

'Yes,' admitted Flavia. 'It's the biggest nose I've ever seen. Why, it's as big as a box!'

82

Jonathan passed along the columned walkway, not looking at the patients, not looking at the doctors, not even pondering Flavia's quest. He was trying to think of a way to get his father and mother to meet. He had not really expected the first stages of his plan to succeed and as a result he had not thought out the later steps very carefully. He was still amazed that his scheme seemed to be working. His first letter had obtained the desired result of an invitation to Rome. And his uncle Simeon was not in Rome, so he must be delivering the second letter, just as Jonathan had asked him to.

Presently Jonathan found himself at the far end of the colonnade, standing before an arched doorway. Stepping through it he saw a small baths complex on his left, public latrines on his right and before him – where the island tapered to its end – another sacred precinct. Like the sanctuary at the front of the island this precinct had a well, an altar, a temple and a tiny grove. But the feel of the place was very different.

This temple was smaller, with black and green marbled columns and a green pediment. The trees around it seemed older, with the poplars, chestnuts and oaks casting darker shadows. And this precinct was oddly deserted. The sun went behind a small cloud and Jonathan shivered as he slowly skirted the altar, mounted the temple steps and peered between the black and green columns into the open door of the cella. In the shadowy interior he saw the cult statue. At first glance it looked like a naked dancing man but as

Jonathan drew closer he saw that the bearded figure had little horns and a goat's tail.

From somewhere in the grove outside the temple came the haunting, breathy sound of shepherd pipes and Jonathan suddenly knew whose shrine this was: Pan. Also known as Faunus. Half man, half goat. Pagan god of the groves. Something about his tail and horns made Jonathan shiver, so he turned and hurried out of the temple and back down the steps.

SCROLL XV

As Jonathan left the Temple of Faunus he noticed something he had not seen before. A room built against the back of the long colonnade, between the latrines and baths. At first glance it looked like a tavern, because it had a wide door with a counter.

Jonathan stepped in and immediately a hundred different smells filled his head. The wall behind the counter was covered with cube-shaped niches, each of which contained a box full of herbs or spices.

And there on the marble-topped counter before him lay all the medical paraphernalia any doctor could ever want: bronze scales, weights, spoons, scoops, probes, needles, tweezers, saws and cupping vessels. Most of the instruments were double-ended. He picked one up, holding it in between the elegant iron scalpel at one end and a bronze probe at the other. It balanced beautifully in his fingers. He replaced it carefully in its soft leather case and moved along the counter.

Here were votive body parts. These little clay images would be dedicated at the temples to remind the god of someone's particular affliction. There were tiny clay feet, hands, ears, noses, eyes, tongues. There were even clay models of the inner and private parts of the body, both male and female.

Moving further along Jonathan found marble mortars and pestles, ceramic ointment pots, leather cylinders, silver plaques, brass votive feathers, muslin sachets of herbs, even lead curse tablets.

And then there were the boxes. Big boxes and little boxes. Boxes made of wood, clay, bronze, even ivory. Some were round, some square, some rectangular.

'Yes please?' A curtain of beads rattled as a young man parted them and stepped into the shop from an inner room. 'May I help you?'

'Are you a doctor?'

'No,' said the young man. 'I am Smintheus, a humble apothecary. I supply the doctors and priests with any supplies they might need.'

'Smintheus? Doesn't that mean "mouse" in Greek?'

'Yes. It means "mouse".'

'I'm Jonathan. My father Mordecai is one of the doctors here at the clinic. I've never heard of half these medicines.' He gestured up at the spice drawers on the wall behind Smintheus and read out their names: 'Absinthe, Acacia Gum, Aloes, Alum, Ambrosia, Anise, Asafoetida, Asclepion . . . what's Asclepion?' he asked.

'Yes please. It is an ointment for the healing of scars.'

'I have a scar.' Jonathan shrugged back his nutmeg-coloured cloak and lifted up his tunic sleeve to show the apothecary his left shoulder.

'Ah,' said Smintheus softly. 'The Emperor's brand.' He leant forward to examine it. 'Five, six months old?'

Jonathan nodded.

'Is it painful?'

'Sometimes.'

Smintheus crouched behind the counter, then rose up again with a small phial of blue glass. He removed a tiny cork stopper and poured a drop of milky ointment onto the palm of his left hand.

'Yes, please,' he said. 'Let me anoint the wound.'

Jonathan closed his eyes as Smintheus gently smoothed some of the cool balm over his brand.

'My father's been using Syrian balm,' said Jonathan after a moment, 'but this one feels better. I don't suppose you have anything for asthma.'

'Of course.' Smintheus turned and stretched up so high that his cream tunic rose up, exposing the backs of his knees. Carefully he eased a box out of its niche and set it on the counter.

'*Ephedron*?' said Jonathan, reading the painted letters. 'I've never heard of it.'

'I'm surprised. It's the best cure for asthma I know.' He pulled out a dried branch with thin twigs sprouting from it, closely bunched and pointing one direction, so that it looked like a small broom.

'It doesn't look like anything special.'

'Ah, but it is. It provides miraculous results.'

'Wait,' said Jonathan. 'It smells familiar.' He lifted the box to his nose and inhaled, then sniffed at the herb pouch around his neck. 'That's it! That's the herb my father has been trying to identify!'

The young man examined Jonathan's herb pouch with interest.

'Where did you get this?'

'A man named Pliny gave it to me last year.'

'Pliny the great naturalist?' Smintheus let go of the pouch. 'The man who died in the eruption?'

'That's the one.'

'But didn't he tell you? To smell *ephedron* is good, but to drink it is one hundred times better.'

'I didn't know that. I don't think my father knows that either. But how do you drink twigs?'

'You boil the branches gently for several hours, then strain the liquid through muslin. The resulting decoction is pale gold. Add seven or eight drops of this liquid to dry red wine and drink it down. It doesn't work as quickly as breathing the herb, but it is much more effective. I know because I myself suffer from asthma. Wait here please.'

The young man turned and disappeared through the bead curtain again.

Jonathan read the names of the herbs for a few moments, then turned his attention to the objects on the counter.

The bead curtain rattled softly again as Smintheus came back in. He put a ceramic jar on the marble counter.

'Yes, please,' he said. '*Ephedron* for you.'

'Thank you,' said Jonathan. 'How much do I—'

'Because you are the doctor's son, no charge,' said Smintheus. 'Our illustrious Emperor pays for everything.'

'Thank you.' Jonathan took the jar and slipped it into his belt pouch. 'Are any of these boxes dangerous?' he asked. 'If you open them, I mean . . .'

'Only this one,' said the young man, indicating a circular box with a lid the diameter of his forearm.

Jonathan bent to examine it and on closer inspection he saw that it was really a basket: tightly woven strips of palm leaves for the base and a looser weave – one which left tiny hexagonal holes – for the lid.

Suddenly he stood up straight.

'Are those . . . air-holes?'

'Yes please.'

Jonathan took a step back. 'So what's in there?'

'My pet cobra. I call him Ptolemy.'

'Diet,' said Egnatius to Lupus. 'Diet is my method of treating the victims. Food is medicine. Did you know that, boy?'

Lupus shook his head and stared at the doctor, whose frizzy hair and tanned skin were exactly the same shade of golden brown. The man looked like a golden statue that had come to life. Even the linen curtains of his patients' cells were pale gold in colour.

'Yes,' said Egnatius, who stood before a wooden table, chopping cabbage. 'Light foods for this, medium foods for that and heavy foods for the other.'

He stopped chopping for a moment and confided in a dramatic whisper: 'Never eat cheese.'

Lupus raised his eyebrows.

'Cheese causes too much phlegm. And fruit is dangerous, too. But cabbage will cure almost anything. And I always tell my patients to eat a raw onion every morning. Crunch it like an apple.' He stopped chopping and looked intently at Lupus. 'Would you like to know my special secret? The best medicine of all?'

Lupus nodded.

Egnatius leaned forward and whispered.

'Urine.'

Lupus opened his eyes wide.

'That's right: urine. It's free. It's yours. Morning urine is best, middle of the stream. Especially if you've eaten lots of cabbage the day before.'

Lupus shook his head slowly in disbelief.

'Really!' said Egnatius, and recited, 'It's good for jaundice, rheumatism, gout, asthma, skin ulcers, burns, wounds, headaches, ear infections, snake bites, baldness, leprosy, obesity, fever, insomnia and fatigue.'

Lupus opened his mouth and pointed inside.

'Oh you poor boy! Your tongue has been cut out! I'm sorry but that's one ailment urine won't help . . .'

Lupus shook his head and pretended to drink from an imaginary beaker.

'Oh! You want to know if you drink the urine? Of course you drink it. But you can also soak your feet in it for ringworm, rub it into your scalp for baldness, and dilute a few drops in water for an eye bath. I also splash some on my cheeks after I've been to the barber. My skin's wonderfully soft. Would you like to feel it?'

Lupus took a step back and shook his head.

'Look at my teeth then.' Egnatius bared his teeth in a grin. 'I use my own urine as a mouthwash. See how white?'

Lupus nodded in wonder. The doctor's teeth were brilliantly white – almost unnaturally so.

'Best of all,' concluded Egnatius, 'is urine taken as a prophylactic, that is to say: a tonic to guard against illness. If you drink a little of your own urine every morning it will protect you wonderfully against pestilence.'

SCROLL XVI

'I think I'd rather have the pestilence,' said Jonathan, reading the notes etched in Lupus's wax tablet.

Lupus nodded, and wrote:

HIS SKIN AND HAIR ARE SAME
COLOUR AS WHAT HE DRINKS

'Ewww!' said Flavia and Nubia giggled behind her hand.

'How about you, Jonathan? Does your doctor think he's one step down from Jupiter?'

'I didn't find a doctor,' said Jonathan, 'but I found an apothecary with lots of boxes. I don't think you'd like him, Nubia. One of the boxes has a snake in it.'

'Why?'

'He says the venom of a snake is the only cure for a snake bite so he has to milk it every day. He gave me this,' added Jonathan, reaching into his belt pouch and pulling out a small clay jar.

'Is it snake milk?' asked Nubia, taking an involuntary step backwards.

'No.' Jonathan smiled. 'It's for my asthma. And he didn't even charge me. He said the Emperor pays for everything.'

'So,' said Flavia, looking around at her three friends. 'Apart from Jonathan, we've *all* found doctors who think they're one step down from Jupiter?'

Lupus nodded emphatically.

'My doctor,' said Nubia carefully, 'thinks he is one step up from Jupiter.'

They all laughed and Lupus gave Nubia a thumbs-up for her joke.

Then Flavia sighed and looked around at them. 'So where does that leave our investigation? Are we any closer to finding our Prometheus? Or are we looking in entirely the wrong place?'

Nubia did not like the black plaster walls of Titus's private winter triclinium, or the small, ghostlike figures painted in white across the lower part of the panels. The scenes made her think of the Land of Grey, the land of the dead. But at least the room was warmer than any of the others she had been in. The black walls seemed to hold the heat from the brazier. She pressed her bare feet against the warm wall and pulled her lionskin cloak tighter round her shoulders. She and Flavia were reclining on the left-hand couch of three. Jonathan and Lupus sat cross-legged on the couch opposite them.

Mordecai reclined on the central couch alone. One of the long-haired slave-boys had washed their hands and feet with warm rose-scented water, and the other had dried them with linen towels.

'Sorry to keep you waiting,' said Titus, striding into the room. 'I'm getting one of my headaches and I've just let blood. It sometimes helps.'

He sat on the central couch beside Mordecai and extended his legs. Instantly the black-haired slave named Biztha removed the imperial sandals and poured water from a silver jug on Titus's feet, catching the overflow deftly with a silver bowl beneath.

'Bigtha,' said Titus to the brown-haired boy who had stepped forward to dry his feet, 'will you bring us some warm mulsum? And tell the serving-girls to bring the first course immediately. I'm ravenous.' He swung his feet up onto the couch and gave Mordecai a distracted smile.

A few minutes later, Titus pushed away his empty plate and said, 'That's better. Now tell me, Jonathan. What progress have you made?'

Nubia saw Jonathan look surprised. He had obviously been miles away. Flavia came to the rescue.

'I can tell you,' she said. 'The mythological Prometheus did more than bring fire to man—'

'Water!' yelled the Emperor, and they all stared at him as Biztha rushed forward with a silver jug. Titus seized the jug and tipped it so that a stream of water spattered onto the marble floor beneath the tables.

'Don't you know,' he said, handing the jug back to the boy, 'that it's bad luck to mention that word at a banquet?'

Flavia frowned. 'What word? "Fire"?'

'WATER!' bellowed Titus again, and again he tipped another stream of water onto the floor.

Nubia giggled behind her hand and Lupus guffawed. But Titus's scowl silenced them and he handed back the jug.

'Proceed,' he commanded Flavia. 'You were telling me what you discovered about Prometheus.'

'Um . . . yes. Well Prometheus brought . . . that hot yellow stuff to man. Although what he did was good for mankind, the gods considered it to be hubris – because he acted as if he knew better than Jupiter. Prometheus also taught mankind about medicine and healing. So we think your prophetic "Prometheus" might be one of the doctors you invited to the clinic on Snake Island. One who thinks he's as good as Jupiter.'

Biztha brought in three platters of cubed meat garnished with watercress and set one before each couch.

'And?' Titus stabbed a piece of meat with the sharp end of his spoon and held it up. Biztha took a step towards his master and his silky hair screened his face as he bent forward, delicately took the piece of meat in his mouth, chewed and then swallowed it.

Nubia tried her own meat. It was roast boar: tender and delicious.

'We haven't come up with the answer yet, Caesar,' said Flavia bravely. 'But we will.'

'Good. I have every confidence in the four of you.' Titus was eating his boar now. 'How about you, doctor? I hear that you've already had remarkable results with your method of treating the fever. Results as good as Cosmus, if not better.'

Mordecai kept his eyes lowered. 'Praise God, my patients are doing well. I believe they are responding to herbal steam.'

Titus held out his cup and Biztha moved forward instantly to refill it.

'My informants say you did not lose a single patient today.'

Mordecai inclined his head. 'I give the glory to God.'

Titus frowned and pressed his knuckles to his fore-head. 'Nubia,' he said presently. 'Do you remember how the three of you played music for me once in the Golden House?'

'Yes, Caesar,' she said softly.

'Did you bring your instruments with you as I requested in my letter?'

'Yes, Caesar.' Nubia wore her flute on a cord round her neck. Now she pulled it out. 'Behold!'

'*Our* instruments are in our rooms,' said Flavia.

'Bigtha, fetch their instruments, please.' Titus continued to massage his wide forehead with his knuckles. 'My head is throbbing as if a blacksmith was beating his anvil in my skull. Your music brought me some relief before. I pray it might do so again.'

The black-walled triclinium was full of golden lamp-light, the smell of roast boar, and vibrant music. Jonathan and his friends were playing a song Nubia had composed: The Storyteller. Jonathan glanced up from his barbiton to see the Emperor's reaction.

It was strange, almost surreal, to see his father re-clining on a couch beside the Emperor Titus. Especially because Jonathan had dined with his mother and the Emperor only the day before. Now here he was with his father and the Emperor: the dark, aristocratic-looking Jew reclining next to the stocky, sandy-haired ex-soldier.

Titus had his head back and his eyes closed but Jonathan noticed that his usually ruddy face was pale and his lips pinched. The music swelled and then came the resolution, with the sound reverberating even after they had played the last note.

Titus opened his eyes, and took a sip of his wine.

'Biztha. Bigtha. Dance for me.' He spoke to the slave-boys, who stood either side of the doorway. And to Nubia, 'Play that first song again. What did you call it? Slave Song?'

Nubia nodded and lifted the flute to her lips.

The slave-boys stripped down to their loincloths and began to dance. For the first time, Jonathan really looked at them. He guessed they were about his age. But unlike him, they had no puppy fat on their lithe, muscular bodies.

Jonathan glanced uneasily at his father, who was staring fixedly down at the couch, and he felt his conscience twinge. What could he have been thinking? Bringing his father here to the inner sanctum of Titus, the great enemy of the Jews?

Suddenly there was a crash, and a sizzling sound. Titus had thrown his cup against the wall beside the doorway and drops had spattered on the red-hot coals of the brazier. The dripping splash mark on the black and grey panels was almost invisible.

'No!' Titus was clutching his head with one hand and pounding the couch with the other. 'It's no good. I can't . . . make it . . . stop!'

SCROLL XVII

'What do you think is wrong with Titus?' Flavia whispered to the others after Mordecai and the slave-boys had followed the Emperor out of the dining-room.

'His headaches, of course,' said Jonathan. 'Father will give him something, maybe the elixir . . .'

Suddenly Flavia's eyes grew wide. 'You don't think someone is trying to poison Titus, do you? Another assassination attempt?'

Lupus had been carefully pouring watered wine down his throat, but at this he coughed and hastily put down his cup.

'He makes his slaves taste his food,' said Jonathan, 'so presumably it's not poisoned.'

'That is why he is feeding Biztha?' asked Nubia. 'In case of the food being poisoned?'

He nodded. 'If the food is poisoned then the slaves die.'

'Jonathan!' breathed Flavia. 'I've just thought of something else; something we should have thought of long before now. After we stopped the assassin last year, you told us that Berenice had an agent in the imperial household—'

'You're right,' said Jonathan. 'Berenice told my uncle that she had an agent in the palace. Someone close to

Titus. She said her agent would be watching. And the assassin would only be paid after he had done the job.'

'Did you ever discover who Berenice's agent was?'

'No.' Jonathan shook his head slowly. 'We never did.'

WHY DIDN'T SHE JUST ASK HER AGENT TO KILL TITUS? Lupus wrote on his wax tablet.

'Titus was never the assassins' target, remember?' said Flavia.

'That's right,' said Jonathan. 'My mother was the one Berenice wanted dead. She hoped that with my mother out of the way Titus might recall her and make her his Empress.'

Lupus used the flat end of his brass stylus to rub out one name and the sharp end to write another.

WHY DIDN'T SHE JUST ASK HER AGENT TO KILL SUSANNAH?

'Good question,' said Jonathan.

They all looked at one another.

'I think I know why,' said Flavia after a few moments. 'Berenice needed – maybe still needs – someone close to the Emperor to tell her what's happening. If anything went wrong and her agent was exposed, she'd be completely in the dark, with no contacts left here in the palace.'

'What if the Berenice is wanting to kill your mother again?' Nubia asked Jonathan.

Flavia gasped. 'Great Neptune's beard, Nubia! You're right. What if "Prometheus" in the prophecy is not a man but a *woman*? What if it's Berenice! Maybe she's so furious with Titus that she wants to destroy Rome! Like Queen Dido, who adored Aeneas at first, but hated him with equal passion after he rejected her love!'

'Berenice often seeks the vengeance,' said Nubia. 'She branded Delilah, the pretty slave-girl who flirts with Titus.'

'And she threw Huldah out of the Golden House just because Titus *looked* at her,' said Flavia.

'Berenice is probably back in Judaea by now,' said Jonathan airily.

'Do we know that for certain?' asked Flavia. 'What if she's come back to Italia in disguise and has hired some more assassins? Or has another evil plan?'

Jonathan frowned. 'No way of knowing,' he said.

'Maybe not,' said Flavia, looking round at their faces. 'But I think I know where we could look for clues.'

THE GOLDEN HOUSE wrote Lupus.

'Exactly!'

'Will we see your friend Rizpah there?' Nubia asked Jonathan.

'Probably. I don't know.'

'I hope we do,' said Flavia. 'I'll bet she could tell us about Berenice. Aren't you worried, Jonathan? That Berenice might still be trying to kill your mother?'

Jonathan was using a roll to mop up the juices of

roast boar. He shrugged. 'Whoever Berenice's agent was, I'm sure he's told her by now.'

'Told her what?' asked Flavia.

'That there's nothing between Titus and my mother. My mother and the Emperor are just friends.'

'Then why was he holding her hand yesterday?' asked Flavia.

'They're just FRIENDS!' shouted Jonathan. Furiously, he kicked away the table with his foot and slid off the dining-couch. 'There's NOTHING between them!'

Flavia, Nubia and Lupus stared open-mouthed as Jonathan stalked out of the black triclinium.

SCROLL XVIII

Nubia's eyes were swollen the following morning and she tried splashing water from the fountain onto her face. But Flavia noticed immediately.

'Have you been crying, Nubia? What's the matter?'

'Venalicius the slave-dealer. All night long he is chasing me in my dreams.'

'But Venalicius is dead. He can't hurt you any more.'

'I know. But he feels alive.' Nubia felt Flavia's arm around her and leaned her head on her friend's shoulder. She tried to stop herself from trembling.

'Poor Nubia,' said Flavia gently. And after a pause, 'I'm sure that was an ivory dream.'

'Ivory?'

Flavia nodded. 'Remember in the *Aeneid*, when the Sibyl takes Aeneas to the underworld? She shows him two gates: one made of horn and one made of ivory. And she tells him that the true dreams come through the gate of horn but the false dreams come through the ivory. You had an ivory dream.'

'But it felt like horn dream,' said Nubia in a small voice.

'Father's just left for Snake Island again,' said Jonathan, coming into the girls' bedroom with Lupus.

'He said he'll be there all day tending the sick. What's the matter, Nubia?'

Nubia couldn't reply.

Flavia said, 'Bad dreams about Venalicius.'

Lupus nodded sympathetically, wrote on his wax tablet and showed it to her:

HE IS DEAD NOW AND
WON'T EVER HURT YOU AGAIN

'But he does still hurt me,' whispered Nubia.

'While we sleep,' came a voice from the doorway, 'the pain we can't forget falls drop by drop upon our hearts . . .'

Nubia and her friends looked up to see Ascletario. He bowed. 'Please to note Aeschylus says that, in his play called *Agamemnon*. Now where would you like me to take you today?'

As they followed Ascletario down the Palatine Hill, Jonathan remembered the joy he had felt when he first discovered his mother was still alive. And the despair – the utter despair – when she had refused to come home with him. She had told him she had a 'calling', that it was her duty to help Titus be a wise ruler. Jonathan knew she was trying to atone for the sin of abandoning her husband and children.

That had been nearly half a year ago, thought Jonathan as he bit into a piece of bread which he had taken from the breakfast table. A person could atone for many sins in six months.

He looked around as it grew brighter. They had left the protection of a long portico and were cutting across a level square.

Ascletario was pointing out the enormous amphitheatre on their right, telling them how tall it was, how many exits it had, how many people it could seat. Parts of the great oval building were still covered in scaffolding and Jonathan knew that the slaves working on it were captives from Jerusalem. Fellow Jews oppressed by Titus. Jonathan tore another angry bite of bread.

While waging war in Judaea, Titus had fallen in love with a beautiful Jewish queen named Berenice. At least some good had come of that unlikely love affair. When the legions under Titus's command finally breached the walls of Jerusalem and stormed the city, Berenice had pleaded with Titus to spare the lives of the inhabitants. He had been merciful. Hundreds had to die in gladiatorial games and in the triumphal parade – that was to be expected – but Titus had sent thousands as slaves to Corinth, to help maintain the isthmus, and thousands more were spared to work on Vespasian's new amphitheatre.

And to please his beautiful Jewish lover, Titus had given Berenice two hundred high-born Jewish women as her handmaids. Including Jonathan's mother. Berenice had installed them in a building so hateful to the people of Rome that no public use could be made of it.

That was where they were going now: Nero's Golden House.

★

Flavia yawned as Ascletario led them down a long corridor of the Golden House.

'Please to note,' said the Egyptian as he trotted along, 'this is only *part* of the so-called Golden House. Nero built it sixteen years ago to be a magnificent setting for his dinner parties. But he died soon after. Later Titus generously allowed the Jewish Queen Berenice to live here with her two hundred handmaidens. Our illustrious Emperor recently set the women free. Many have gone and there are only a few left in this wing. The Golden House will become a school to train gladiators.'

Lupus raised his eyebrows in interest.

'May I ask who are you investigating today?' Ascletario bowed.

'Berenice,' said Flavia.

Ascletario stopped short. 'But she is gone, vanished, departed. Our illustrious Emperor sent her far away.'

'Yes,' said Flavia patiently. 'But we want to look for clues in her bedroom.'

'Desolated, desolated, desolated. Her quarters are off-limits. No persons are allowed there.'

Lupus reached into the neck hole of his tunic and found the ivory pass. He held it out at the full stretch of the cord.

'That won't be any use in this case.' Ascletario bobbed his head and rubbed his hands in abject apology.

'But it's an all-areas pass,' protested Flavia.

'Please to note that Berenice herself decreed her quarters off-limits; even to the Emperor. Besides, her rooms are locked and she took the key, the key, the key.'

They suddenly heard the echoing sound of running footsteps and looked up to see one of Titus's slave-boys, the brown-haired one. Flavia thought it was the one called Bigtha.

'Ascletario,' he gasped. 'Come quickly. Caesar wants you to read the portents.'

'Has something happened?'

Bigtha nodded. 'It's his daughter Julia. She's ill. She has the fever!'

Ascletario looked almost relieved. 'You must excuse me,' he said to Flavia and her friends. 'I humbly bow.'

He backed away, bowing with each step, then turned and trotted down the long corridor after Bigtha.

The four friends looked at each other.

'I didn't know Titus had a daughter,' said Jonathan, scratching his curly head.

'What now?' said Flavia. 'How will we find Berenice's quarters?'

Lupus was writing on his wax tablet.

RIZPAH?

'Yes!' cried Flavia. 'There's bound to be a secret tunnel into Berenice's rooms and according to you, Jonathan, Rizpah knows them all. She's our only hope of getting in there. How can we find her?'

Jonathan shrugged. 'You don't find Rizpah,' he said. 'She usually finds you.'

'He's right,' said a little girl's voice from behind them. 'And you've just been found.'

★

'Rizpah!' cried Jonathan, and then laughed as the little girl threw her arms around his waist. She drew back shyly before he could hug her back and he felt a pang of guilt. They had been in Rome for well over a day and he had barely thought about her. 'How long have you been spying on us?' He pretended to be stern.

Rizpah gazed up at him solemnly. 'Since you came here to the Golden House,' she said.

'You should have come out sooner.'

Rizpah's fine white hair flicked back and forth as she shook her head. 'I don't trust that astrologer.'

'Ascletario?'

Rizpah nodded. 'Why do you want to go to Queen Berenice's quarters?'

'We're trying to solve a mystery and we need some clues,' said Flavia.

Jonathan smiled. 'Rizpah, these are the friends I told you about: Flavia, Nubia and that, of course, is Lupus.'

'The Emperor wants us to solve a prophetic mystery,' said Flavia. ' "When a Prometheus opens a Pandora's box, Rome will be devastated." '

Lupus had been circling Rizpah, examining her from different angles. Tentatively he reached out and fingered a strand of her hair. Rizpah flinched and Lupus jumped back, too. They stared warily at one another for a moment, then Rizpah turned back to Flavia.

'I am not sure,' she said, 'what a Pandora's box is. But there is a special box in Berenice's room. One that must not be opened.' She looked at Jonathan. 'You will be amazed.'

★

'It is beautiful,' breathed Nubia.

Rizpah had disappeared into one of her tunnels and a few minutes later she had opened Berenice's door from the inside.

Now Nubia followed her friends into the room. The space around them was suffused with a golden glow, as if they stood in the middle of a cool yellow flame.

Nubia barely noticed the wide low bed with its head against the right-hand wall. She didn't see the gold and ivory chairs, the beautiful tapestry of scarlet, purple, blue, and white. All she saw was an object illuminated by a circular glass skylight.

It was a beautiful golden chest.

She took a step towards it. She had seen objects covered in gold before, but nothing like this. Perhaps it was the pearly light, pouring down from above. Or the fact that three of the four walls in the room were painted gold. Whatever it was, the box seemed to be the source of the light.

As Nubia took another step forward, she felt her face grow hot. Then warmth flooded her whole body. Was the source of the heat the golden box? Did it have special powers? Nubia knelt before it and reached out to touch it. Her fingertips almost touched the smooth gold surface.

'Stop, Nubia!' cried Jonathan. 'Don't touch it!'

'What?' She turned reluctantly to look at him.

Jonathan looked at Rizpah. 'It's the ark, isn't it?'

Rizpah nodded.

'Ark?' said Flavia. 'What's an ark?'

'The ark of the covenant,' breathed Jonathan. 'From the Temple of God in Jerusalem. If you touch it you will die.'

SCROLL XIX

'Tell us, Jonathan,' said Flavia. 'What on earth is an ark?'

They had shut and bolted the door, and the five of them were sitting on the creamy fleeces which covered Berenice's wide bed. They gazed down at the golden box before them.

'Ark is just another word for box. But this box is special. If it really is the ark. It was made of acacia wood and covered with pure gold, and inside the priests placed Aaron's rod, a jar full of manna and the two stone tablets engraved with the ten commandments. They were meant to remind the Jewish people of all the things God had done for them. The staff to remind them of how God brought them out of Egypt, the manna to remind them of how he looked after them in the desert, and the tablets to remind them of how he would look after them in the promised land.'

'So those things are in that box?' Nubia asked.

Jonathan nodded.

'But if those good things are in the box, then why is it dangerous?' asked Flavia.

'Because it's so holy. So pure.'

Lupus waved his hand to attract their attention. He pretended to touch the ark and then mimicked a man dying. He clutched his throat and crossed his eyes and fell choking back onto the bed.

They all laughed nervously.

'That's right,' said Jonathan. 'Once, long ago, our enemies captured the ark and they all got boils and tumours and died of the plague until they sent the ark back to Israel.'

'Ugh!' Flavia's smile faded. 'It's good you didn't touch it, Nubia. Boils are sores on your skin and tumours are lumps inside you.'

Nubia shuddered.

'Later,' continued Jonathan, 'King David started to take the ark back to Jerusalem on a cart. But they didn't do it properly and a man called Uzzah reached out and touched it and died!'

'That must be why Berenice forbade anyone to come in here,' said Flavia.

'But wouldn't the Berenice be afraid to come in?' Nubia asked.

Lupus and Rizpah nodded.

'No,' said Jonathan. 'Because any Jew who had it in his house was blessed in every way.'

'So it's all right to *have* it,' said Flavia, 'just not to touch it.'

Jonathan nodded.

'If touching it is bad,' said Flavia after a moment, 'I wonder what opening the box would do?'

Lupus clutched his throat and they all nodded grimly.

' "When a Prometheus opens a Pandora's box, Rome will be devastated",' quoted Flavia, and then mused, 'but the plague is already killing thousands and this ark is shut. Do you think it's been opened and closed and that's what caused the plague?'

'Maybe we have to open it to stop plague,' said Nubia softly.

They all looked at the golden box and then at one another.

'Any volunteers?' said Jonathan.

They all shook their heads and suddenly Nubia cried:

'Hark! Voices are coming!'

'This isn't a very good hiding place,' Jonathan whispered to Flavia. The five friends were crouching behind the far side of the bed.

'I know. But it's the only place in the room,' she hissed back.

They heard the sound of a large key being inserted in its hole, pushing the bolt up, pulling it back. Jonathan heard a man's voice from the doorway.

'Purify the room with incense, wipe down the walls and floors,' he said. 'Clean the bedding and dust everything. But don't touch the curtain. Or the box. Do you understand?'

'I understand,' came a soft female voice. Probably a slave-girl, thought Jonathan.

'Hurry and get the cleaning things now,' said the man's voice again. It was a husky, well-educated voice, and although it was maddeningly familiar, Jonathan couldn't match it to a face. 'I want everything to be perfect for Berenice when she returns.'

Berenice! Jonathan turned to look at Flavia wide-eyed, but she gazed back blankly.

Then he realised that the man and the slave-girl had been speaking in Hebrew.

'What were they saying?' Flavia asked Jonathan.

After Mystery-voice and the slave-girl had left, the five friends had managed to slip out of Berenice's room. Now they were hiding in an alcove off the corridor behind a large marble statue of a Trojan and his sons being devoured by sea serpents.

'Who was the man at the door?' said Flavia. 'His voice sounded familiar . . .'

Lupus wrote a name on his wax tablet and showed it to them:

AGATHUS.

'That's right,' said Rizpah. 'He is Titus's chief steward.'

'Of course!' said Jonathan. 'I should have recognised his voice.'

'What did he say?' asked Flavia.

'He told the slave-girl to tidy the room. I think she'll be back in a minute. He also told her not to touch the box.'

'Then it must be the ark,' breathed Flavia. 'It must be Pandora's box. What now?'

FIND OUT MORE ABOUT THE ARK wrote Lupus on his wax tablet.

Flavia nodded. 'And we need to find out more about Berenice! I think she's a better suspect than the doctors. What is it, Jonathan? What are you whispering to Rizpah?'

'Nothing,' said Jonathan. 'Er . . . why don't I ask my mother if she knows anything?'

'Good idea. Nubia and I will do research in the library of the Temple of Apollo. That man Josephus probably knows a lot about Berenice and the ark. Lupus, you and Rizpah are small enough to hide in the tunnels. Can you stay here and snoop around and tell us if you get any more information? Find out why the slave-girl is cleaning the room now? Maybe Berenice is planning to come back . . .'

'But didn't you—' Rizpah frowned at Jonathan.

'Shhh!' said Jonathan. 'Do I hear someone coming? No. I guess not. No,' he said again, giving Rizpah a hard look.

Lupus wrote on his wax tablet and showed it to Flavia.

WHERE WILL YOU BE, he wrote, IF WE FIND OUT ANYTHING?

'Let's meet in the Latin colonnade of the Temple of Apollo,' she whispered. 'It's about the fourth hour now, so make it noon – in two hours. If any of us finds any information and can't be there at that time, just leave a message on a wax tablet. We'll have to use a simple code . . . I know! Greek letters instead of Latin. Use *beta* for V and *eta* for H. And write backwards. It's simple enough to decipher but it will look like nonsense to anyone who might casually glance at it. Do you all understand?'

They nodded.

'Shhh!' whispered Rizpah. 'Here comes Abigail to clean Berenice's room.'

They all held their breath and crouched down behind the statue's base. They heard the slosh of water in a bucket and the almost soundless pad of the slave-girl's feet passing along the corridor. The sound of the key lifting the bolt and the door to Berenice's room opening and then closing.

'Now!' hissed Flavia. 'Let's go!'

'Shalom, Titus Flavius Josephus,' said Flavia politely. 'Peace be with you.'

The bearded man glanced up from his scrolls and sheets of papyrus and his face relaxed as he saw the girls standing before him.

'Flavia Gemina, isn't it?' he said. 'Have a seat.'

'Thank you. And this is my friend Nubia.'

'Shalom, Nubia. How may I help you girls?' he asked as they pulled back chairs and sat across from him. 'Do you need help translating your Aeschylus?'

'No,' said Flavia. 'But can you tell us about the ark of the covenant?'

'The ark?' His heavy eyebrows lifted in surprise.

'Yes. What happened to it after the Temple was destroyed? Did Titus bring it back to Rome?'

'Not at all,' he said. 'After Titus destroyed the temple

he sent some men to find the ark. We found the great menorah – the lampstand – and many other holy implements. But of the ark we found no trace.'

SCROLL XX

'Why wasn't the ark in the Temple?' Flavia Gemina asked Flavius Josephus.

'There are several theories,' he replied, stroking his beard. 'Some believe it was taken away by the Queen of Sheba in Solomon's time. Others think that when the King of Babylon was besieging Jerusalem it was hidden in a maze of secret tunnels beneath the First Temple, and that it lies there still.'

'Like a labyrinth!' breathed Flavia. 'But with a holy treasure instead of a minotaur.'

'What is First Temple?' Nubia asked Josephus.

'We Jews call the temple built by Solomon the First Temple. It was destroyed on the ninth of Av and our people sent into exile, to Babylon.'

'Babylon! That's where Jonathan's father comes from.'

'Yes,' said Josephus. 'The Jews who went to Babylon prospered. A thriving community exists there to this day. But not all of our people remained there. Some returned to Jerusalem seventy years after Solomon's temple was destroyed. Seven and seventy are the numbers of completion,' he explained. 'The returning exiles built another temple on the site of the first, which they called the Second Temple. And now I will tell you something amazing: the Second Temple was destroyed by Titus on the ninth of Av, the exact same day of the year that the First Temple was destroyed!'

Flavia felt a delicious shiver down her backbone. 'But the First Temple was destroyed a long time before the Second Temple?'

'Of course,' said Josephus. Then he glanced round to make sure they weren't overheard and leaned forward across the marble table top. 'Many Jews believe the year we are in now will be an evil one, too.'

'Why?' whispered Flavia.

'Because Solomon's temple – the First Temple – was destroyed exactly 666 years ago. That number has significance for us, too.'

'What?' said Flavia.

'It is the number of the Beast.'

Jonathan climbed the stairs which led to the upper level of the Imperial Palace. He was trying to remember the route they taken the previous evening. Agathus had led them along a corridor with a blue-grey marble floor, through a courtyard with a triple fountain, up some stairs, down a corridor with yellow columns, and finally down the corridor with the red porphyry columns.

His heart was pounding and he knew it was not just because he had been climbing stairs. Berenice was on her way, just as he had planned. Soon she would see for herself that Titus and his mother were not lovers. Then his mother would finally be safe. And maybe, when

Titus came face to face with Berenice, he would fall in love with her again.

Jonathan stopped to drink at the fountain with three marble dolphins. The sun had appeared from behind a cloud. He closed his eyes and tilted his head back, enjoying its gentle warmth on his face as his heart-beat returned to normal. The clink of armour made him open his eyes and he saw three figures appear at the foot of a stairway on the other side of the court-yard.

'Father!' he cried. 'What are you doing here?'

Mordecai stopped and turned and the two guards on either side of him stopped, too.

Jonathan ran forward. 'What's happened? Why are you here?' His heart was racing again. 'Have they arrested you?'

'No, no.' His father gave him a tired smile. 'The Emperor's daughter Julia. She came down with the fever this morning. He asked me to treat her.'

'Will she be all right?' asked Jonathan.

Mordecai nodded. 'I think so.'

'So you've been here all morning?' said Jonathan. 'Here on the Palatine Hill?'

'Yes,' said Mordecai. 'Does that surprise you?'

'No,' said Jonathan hastily. 'I'm not surprised. I'm glad. Are you going to stay here today – in the palace, I mean?'

'No.' Mordecai nodded at the guards. 'They're escorting me back to the Tiber Island.' He patted Jonathan's shoulder. 'Don't wait for me this afternoon. I may not be back for dinner.'

Jonathan listened to their footsteps recede down the marble stairs and he gazed thoughtfully out into the bright courtyard.

'I'm not surprised,' he said to himself. 'It's the most natural thing in the world that Titus would want the best doctor in Rome to treat someone he cares for. Why didn't I think of that before?'

'The Beast?' Nubia whispered to Josephus. 'What is the Beast?'

She suddenly noticed tiny drops of sweat on Josephus's forehead, although it was quite cold in the library.

'The Beast?' said Josephus with a frown. 'Were we talking about the Beast?'

'Yes,' said Flavia. 'You were telling us that the ark might have been hidden before the destruction of the First Temple 666 years ago. The number of the Beast? But what is the Beast?'

'Some say Nero, who set the fire. The Hebrew letters of his name add up to 666. Others say Titus, a second Nero. And of the rock badger you may not eat.'

Nubia and Flavia glanced at one another.

'The beast is rock badger?' asked Nubia.

Josephus leaned forward. 'A puppy followed me home once,' he confided in a loud whisper, 'when I was a boy. But my parents would not let me keep him. They said he was an unclean creature.'

'That is very sad,' said Nubia, aware that the imperial scribes at nearby tables were looking at them.

And Flavia added, 'We're sorry your parents

wouldn't let you keep the puppy. But what about the ark?'

Josephus frowned, shook his head and rose unsteadily to his feet. 'The ark is golden and the Beast is not a puppy.' He looked down at Nubia with fevered eyes. 'I touched it! Do you understand?'

She nodded up at him, although she had no idea what he meant, or why he was talking to her and not to Flavia. The silence told her that everyone in the library had stopped reading in order to listen.

'And now I am unclean,' Josephus cried. 'Unclean! Unclean!' He began swatting the air around his face. 'Flies! I can't stand the buzzing. It's the flies. No! It's the . . . rock badger!'

And with those words, he fell to the floor, unconscious.

In the apothecary's storeroom on Snake Island, Smintheus looked at Jonathan and arched one eyebrow. 'You want a potion to make it look as if you have the fever?'

'That's right,' said Jonathan. 'Do you have anything like that?'

'No person has ever asked for such a thing before. Let me think.'

Jonathan nodded and glanced over his shoulder, out through the doorway behind him. It was almost noon. He needed to get back to the Palatine soon, before Flavia and the others began to wonder where he was.

'Eureka!' said Smintheus suddenly. 'I have it. The

tonic I have in mind does not exactly mimic the appearance of fever and chills, but it will put you into a very deep sleep, a sleep closely resembling death. Will that do?'

'I suppose that would work.'

'It is strong medicine. Will you tell me what you want it for?'

Jonathan thought quickly. 'Father wants to see whether some of the doctors can tell the difference between a real fever and a false one. I volunteered to help him. I'll be under his care the whole time.'

'So it is you who will be taking the potion?'

'Yes,' Jonathan lied.

'Very well. I will go and seek.' He disappeared through the bead curtain to a back room. Presently he reappeared with a small clay jar stopped with a tiny cork.

Smintheus held out the small jar and Jonathan took it. It was heavy for its size and had a simple garland of black glazed flowers painted around its terracotta belly. Smintheus wrote something on a papyrus label.

'Tell your father these are the main ingredients. He will know what they are. I suggest you put twenty drops into a cup of sweet red wine and drink it all down,' said Smintheus. 'Within half an hour you will fall into a deep sleep. You will wake after one day – a day and a half at the most – feeling better than ever. Ask your father to come and consult me if he wants to know more.'

Jonathan took the jar and nodded. 'There's no risk of her . . . me taking too much?'

'No,' said Smintheus with a smile. 'Not if you follow the recommended dose. Twenty drops.'

Lupus emerged from the cryptoporticus Rizpah had showed him and brushed off the cobwebs. Then his eyes opened in surprise. Apart from a pair of cooing pigeons, the colonnade of the Latin library was completely deserted. He peered across the courtyard into the Greek library. Also empty.

Lupus shrugged, opened his wax tablet, thought for a moment and wrote:

ΛΛΙ ΑΠΖΙΡ
ΚΝΙΘ Ι ΡΕΒΕΦ
ΠΛΕΗ ΤΕΓ ΟΤ ΔΑΗ

When he had finished writing the coded message he left the wax tablet on the table and went to try to find his friends.

'Mother, you look tired.'
    'Do I?'
    'Yes. You definitely look tired.'
    'I suppose I haven't been sleeping terribly well these past few months.'
    'Why not? Are you worried about something?'
    Susannah gave Jonathan a sad smile. 'I worry about many things. About how you and your sister are doing. About how I betrayed your father. And most of all, about Titus.'

Jonathan felt an unpleasant twist in his stomach. 'Why? What about Titus?'

'I'm afraid he's slipping into his old ways. I thought I was having some influence. But these fits of rage . . .'

'He hasn't hurt you, has he?'

'No, no. He never strikes me. Sometimes he shouts, but he always apologises afterwards.'

'Flavia thinks someone might be poisoning him.'

'I don't think it's poison. I think it's just his nature. His real nature.' She bit her lip and looked away. 'Next month,' she said, 'Titus intends to open the amphitheatre with a hundred days of games. Thousands of gladiators will fight and die. Not to mention the beast fighters and the poor animals. So many innocent men and animals condemned to death. I've realised we are very different in our ways of seeing life.'

'Mother,' said Jonathan carefully. 'If you aren't helping Titus be a better ruler . . . Would you ever reconsider coming home, coming back to Ostia—'

'Jonathan. Even if I wanted to, your father could never forgive me for what I did. Never.'

'But he could, mother. I know he could!'

'No!' She turned away and pressed her fingertips against her forehead. 'Please don't start again, Jonathan. I'm so tired.'

'See? You're tired!' Jonathan took a deep breath. 'Mother, listen to me. I have something for you. This little jar has a tonic in it. If you mix twenty drops in some sweet red wine it will help you get some sleep. Promise me you'll try it.'

'Very well, my son.' She turned and laid a cool hand against his cheek and smiled. 'Perhaps I'll take it tomorrow evening for the Sabbath, our day of rest.'

SCROLL XXI

'Jonathan!' cried Flavia. 'Where have you been? It's an hour past noon.'

'I'm sorry,' he said. 'I came as soon as I could.'

'Did you talk to your mother? Does she have any more information about Berenice or the ark?'

'Er . . . no. Nothing new. Did you talk to Josephus?'

'Yes. He says when Titus captured Jerusalem the soldiers looked for the ark but never found it. Josephus thinks it's still buried in a secret labyrinth underneath where the Temple used to be.'

'He doesn't think there's any chance the gold box in Berenice's room could be the ark?'

'We didn't get that far,' said Flavia. 'The fever got him and he collapsed dramatically. In fact, I'm not sure how much of what he told us was delirious ranting.'

'Where's Lupus?'

'We don't know. He's probably looking for us. After Josephus collapsed all the scribes ran out of the library and we went to find a doctor. When we got back the library was deserted. But Lupus must have come because he wrote on this wax tablet.'

Jonathan picked up the coded tablet and sounded out the words as he read it backwards:

'Rizpa . . . ill . . . feber?'

'Greek has no V,' said Flavia. 'Remember we agreed to substitute *beta*?'

'Oh, fever!' said Jonathan, and continued decoding. 'Rizpah ill . . . Fever I think . . . had . . . to get . . . help.' He looked up at Flavia and Nubia. 'Poor Rizpah.'

Flavia nodded grimly. 'They're dropping like flies!' she said, and then, 'Oh, Nubia! Don't cry! I know what would cheer you up. Shall we go to the baths this afternoon?'

Nubia nodded.

'We can go to the new Baths of Titus. They're close to the Golden House, so we might pick up some good gossip about Berenice. Do you want to come, too, Jonathan? You can do the men's quarters and we'll do the ladies' section.'

'I suppose,' said Jonathan. 'I haven't been to the baths since we got to Rome.'

'Behold! Lupus is coming,' said Nubia through her tears.

'Good,' said Flavia. 'Now we can all go over to the baths together.'

'Well, the baths were a wash-out,' said Flavia to the others over breakfast on the following morning. 'The floor of the frigidarium was so oily I almost slipped and broke my neck.'

Nubia nodded. 'The hot plunge was not hot,' she said.

'And that's the worst criticism Nubia can give,' laughed Flavia.

'There was something disgusting floating on the surface of the water in our caldarium,' said Jonathan. 'It was lucky Lupus spotted it. Also, half the men there were sick: coughing and spitting. It's good we've already had the fever.'

'I want to go home,' said Nubia in a small voice. 'I want to go to the Baths of Thetis and see Nipur and eat what Alma cooks.'

'The Emperor has just sent us a message inviting us to dinner this afternoon,' said Flavia. 'He's probably going to ask us what we've discovered. I think we can go home if we've solved the mystery by then. So what do we think? Who is our Prometheus? Give me your theories.'

'I think the Prometheus is doctor named Diaulus,' said Nubia. 'He brings more sickness because he takes blood from those already weak. Pandora's box is the box he calls his "wound box". Titus should send him far, far away.'

'That's a reasonable theory . . .' said Flavia. 'Why are you shaking your head, Lupus?'

Lupus held out his wax tablet. On it he had written:

PANDORA'S BOX MUST BE THE ARK
I THINK JOSEPHUS OPENED IT
TO LET THE PLAGUE OUT
THAT'S WHY HE GOT THE FEVER.
HE IS PROMETHEUS

'Interesting,' said Flavia thoughtfully. 'The conquered Jew is willing to die in order to bring destruction upon the city and people who destroyed *his* city and people. That's an excellent theory, Lupus. But I think mine is the best. The only problem is it might get me executed.'

They all looked at her.

Flavia lowered her voice. 'I think Titus himself is Prometheus. And that by destroying Jerusalem and burning the Second Temple he opened a kind of Pandora's box: Mount Vesuvius! It has caused death and blight and pestilence for the last half year. I think Jonathan's god must be like Jupiter, only even more powerful because he made the volcano erupt to punish Titus and the Roman people.' Flavia sat back, pleased, and looked at Jonathan. 'What do you think of my theory, Jonathan?'

Jonathan shrugged and took another piece of cheese and a handful of dried figs. 'Not bad.'

'Who do you think Prometheus is?'

'I don't know who Prometheus is.'

'Then what's your theory?'

'I don't have one.'

'Don't you care if Rome is devastated?'

'Actually . . .' said Jonathan, washing down his last mouthful with barley water and wiping his mouth with the back of his hand, 'no. I don't care if Rome is devastated. All I care about is getting my father back together with my mother, so that she can come home.' The bronze chair grated on the mosaic floor as he pushed it back from the table and stood. 'I'm tired of waiting and waiting and of nothing happening. I've decided to do something about it.'

'Jonathan!' said Flavia catching his wrist. 'You can't. You promised your mother.'

'How can *you* – of all people – say that to me?' said Jonathan, looking down at her. 'You disobey your father whenever it suits you, so why can't I disobey my mother this one time? It's for her own good.'

'Because you're better than I am. You're obedient and good and honest. That's who you are.'

'And where has it got me?' He shook off her hand. 'Nowhere. I don't care about the stupid prophecy! I only care about bringing my mother back home. Besides,' he said, as he went out of the room, 'you don't even know what I plan to do.'

'*I* don't even know what I plan to do,' Jonathan muttered to himself.

His feet were taking him towards the part of the palace where his mother had her rooms. What if she hadn't waited until the Sabbath but had already taken his tonic and lay apparently struck down by the fever? Maybe Titus had found her and had already sent for the best doctor in Rome: Mordecai ben Ezra. But what if the Emperor had summoned another doctor who would bleed her or make her drink some horrible concoction? Or what if she had taken too much and they thought she was dead? It suddenly occurred to him that the sleeping potion was a very bad idea.

His mother had said she might take the potion this evening and it was only morning. But he had a sudden stab of doubt and so he quickened his pace. Something told him he should warn his mother not to take the potion after all.

SCROLL XXII

As Jonathan hurried across a bright morning court-yard, he saw his father coming towards him. Mordecai had his medical bag over his shoulder and was ob-viously lost in thought. He was coming from Julia's rooms and this time he was alone.

One chance meeting was coincidence. Two must be by divine appointment. Suddenly Jonathan knew what he had to do.

'Father!' he called. 'Good morning.' His own voice sounded strangely confident.

'Jonathan!' said his father in surprise. 'How are you? Have you solved the Emperor's mystery yet?'

'No,' said Jonathan, waving his hand dismissively. 'It's a stupid prophecy. It's just his imagination.'

Mordecai smiled. 'Don't share that opinion with Titus. He takes these things very seriously. I've just been with him and his daughter,' he continued. 'Praise God: Julia's fever broke this morning and she's going to be fine. Have you had breakfast? Which way are you going?'

Jonathan took a deep breath. 'I'm going this way, father. And I think you should come with me. I have something to show you. Something important.'

★

Lupus thoughtfully poured the last of the buttermilk down his throat. He was worried about Jonathan.

As if Flavia had read his mind, she said, 'Has anyone else noticed how grumpy Jonathan has been lately?

'Jonathan is missing his mother,' said Nubia.

Lupus nodded his agreement.

'It must be hard for him,' said Flavia, 'knowing his mother is alive but not being able to tell his father.'

'It must be hard for him,' echoed Nubia, 'because his father and mother are so close but cannot meet.'

'Did it ever occur to you,' said Flavia slowly, 'how odd it is that the Emperor should invite Mordecai here to Rome just a few months after Jonathan discovered his mother was alive?'

Suddenly Lupus knew. He uttered a strangled grunt of excitement.

Flavia and Nubia automatically slapped his back but he waved them off impatiently and wrote on his wax tablet:

SOMEONE WROTE TO TITUS ABOUT
MORDECAI

'That's right,' said Flavia. 'The Emperor said he got a letter telling how Mordecai has been curing lots of people in Ostia.'

LATE ONE NIGHT wrote Lupus
ABOUT A WEEK AGO
I SAW JONATHAN WRITING A LETTER
AND HE SIGNED IT WITH TITUS'S SEAL

'Great Juno's peacock!' cried Flavia. 'It was Jonathan who wrote the letter to Titus. He's the one who got us all invited!'

Lupus nodded.

'But why?' said Flavia.

'He wants mother and father to meet,' said Nubia.

'Of course!' said Flavia, hitting her forehead with the heel of her hand. 'I'm so stupid. I should have figured it out a long time ago.'

'He is promising his mother not to tell about father . . .' began Nubia.

Scribbling furiously, Lupus finished her thought:

BUT HE DIDN'T PROMISE NOT TO BRING HIM TO HER!

'And Mordecai is probably here in the palace again today, treating Titus's daughter!' cried Flavia.

They all looked at one another.

'Come on!' cried Flavia. 'Let's find Jonathan and stop him doing something he might regret!'

'Are you finally taking me to her?' said Mordecai as he walked beside Jonathan down the polished corridor.

'Yes, she's this way . . .' said Jonathan. And then stopped, his heart beating hard. His father had stopped, too, and they stood staring at one another.

'What do you mean?' asked Jonathan.

'Your mother. Susannah. Are you finally taking me to her?'

For a moment Jonathan seemed to see a stranger. A

tall, dark-eyed Roman in a white tunic and blue woollen cloak, his leather medical bag over one shoulder, standing framed between two deep red porphyry columns.

'You know mother's alive?' Jonathan managed to say. 'How?'

'You told me.'

'No . . . I never . . . When did I tell you?'

'When you had the fever, after the Saturnalia. You said things . . . things that made me suspect. You spoke of her. Of Titus and Berenice, too . . .'

'Mother made me promise not to tell you.'

'Don't worry.' His father gazed down the corridor, towards the double doors at the end. 'You were delirious. You didn't break your promise.'

'Father . . . do you think you could love her again?'

His father was silent.

'I suppose now you love that widow – Helena Aurelia,' Jonathan said miserably, 'with her silvery laugh.'

Jonathan's father turned to look at him. 'In my whole life,' he said quietly, 'your mother is the only woman I have ever loved.'

'But could you forgive her? Take her back?'

'In a heartbeat.'

'Then let me take you to her.'

SCROLL XXIII

Jonathan pulled the double doors open for his father but remained hidden behind the right-hand one, so that his mother would not see him. Then, heart pounding, he put his eye to the crack.

His mother sat on a chair before the loom. She was weaving and her head was turned to speak to Delilah, who sat on a floor cushion sorting balls of wool. Beams of morning sunlight shone through the lattice-work screen of the window, stamping bright hexagons of red, green and blue on the coloured web of wool. As Mordecai moved into Jonathan's line of sight, Susannah looked up towards the doorway.

'Who are you?' she said, rising to her feet and taking a step backwards. She wore a long shift of peacock blue and her hair was tied back. 'What do you want with me?' She spoke in Latin.

Delilah had risen from her cushion and stood protectively beside her mistress.

'Susannah. Don't you know me?' He spoke softly, in Hebrew.

She looked at him, her eyes huge.

'Mordecai?'

He nodded and smiled.

'But you look so different . . . Where's your beard?

You . . . Dear God!' She dropped her head in her hands. 'I knew this would happen.' Her voice was muffled. 'I never wanted you to see me. Please go away!'

'Susannah, I know what you've been through.' He took a step towards her. 'Can you forgive me?'

'Can I forgive *you*?' She lifted her face and Jonathan saw that her eyes were filled with tears. 'I should be begging *your* forgiveness. You were a good man. A good husband. And I betrayed you.'

'Susannah,' he took another step towards her, 'please forgive me for not taking you with me when I left Jerusalem.'

'I refused to go.'

'And I let you refuse . . . I think part of me suspected that you loved someone else. I was a coward. I wasn't willing to fight for you. I'm so sorry, Susannah. Sorry for what you had to endure. It must have been awful.'

'It was my own fault.'

'Still, it must have been terrible for you.'

The tears that had been brimming spilled down her cheeks. 'It was,' she was still speaking in Hebrew, 'the disease, the famine, the crucifixions . . . I watched my parents slowly die of hunger. And there was nothing I could do. Oh, Mordecai, I've never felt so helpless.' Jonathan held his breath as his father eased his medical bag from his shoulder to the floor and moved towards her.

'Susannah,' he said. 'My dear wife. It's over now. You've atoned for your sins.'

'Can God really forgive me?'

'Yes.' He stopped in front of her.

'And can you?' she whispered.

'I forgave you long ago,' he said softly, and opened his arms.

'Oh Mordecai!' She moved forward, weeping, into his embrace.

Jonathan's father had bent his face to kiss the top of her head and his words were muffled.

'Kiss her properly,' muttered Jonathan to himself as a great foolish grin spread across his face. An intense happiness was flooding his heart. His plan had worked. All they had to do now was—

'YOU!' cried a man's voice, full of fury.

Jonathan whirled to see a figure standing in the corridor behind him.

It was the Emperor Titus.

SCROLL XXIV

Titus stood in the corridor a few paces from the open doorway, his square face flushed with anger.

'How DARE you!' the Emperor roared.

He was not addressing Mordecai, who stood with his arms around his long-lost wife.

Nor was he addressing Susannah, who had not pulled away from her husband's embrace.

The Emperor was glaring at Jonathan.

'How dare you bring your father here against her wishes and mine!'

'Forgive me, Emperor! I mean Caesar . . . I thought my mother might be ill. I thought—'

'Liar!' cried Titus, moving swiftly forward. He gripped Jonathan's ear, pulling him roughly out from behind the door and into the room. Then he pushed Jonathan down onto the floor at Susannah's feet.

'This is your doing. Apologise to your mother!'

Jonathan found himself on hands and knees. The rough edges of the mosaic floor had cut him, and his hands left smears of blood as he wiped them on his cream tunic and struggled to his feet.

'I'm sorry, mother.' He could not bring himself to look at her.

But he looked up when Titus addressed his father.

'And you! You have abused my hospitality, Jew,' he said. 'I conferred citizenship upon you, opened my palace to you, entrusted the life of my daughter to your care . . . And what do you do? You make love to my consort.'

'Your *what*?' Susannah stared at Titus, aghast.

'She may be your consort,' said Mordecai in his accented Latin. 'But she is my wife.'

'Impudent!' Titus drew back his hand and with a powerful blow he knocked Jonathan's father to the floor. 'I could have you beheaded in an instant,' he said. 'She is not your wife. She is a slave. *My* slave. And I say you will not have her!'

Mordecai struggled to his feet, one side of his face red where he had been struck.

He was shaking but he deliberately presented Titus with his other cheek.

Titus furiously raised his hand, then let it drop. His shoulders slumped.

'You love her, too, don't you?' said Mordecai quietly.

'No, Mordecai,' said Susannah. 'It's not like that. Please tell him, Titus. Tell him we're just friends. Tell him you don't love me.'

'Of course I love you!' Titus cried, rounding on Susannah. He was still breathing hard, but his face was losing its angry flush. He gazed at her. 'What did you think? I've tried to pretend, to convince myself that I come to you for advice, for support . . . But seeing you in his arms like that made me realise.' He took her hands in his. 'Susannah, I love you more than anything in the world. I believe you are the only good thing that has ever come into my life.'

'No,' said Jonathan, raising both hands and taking a step back. 'You can't love her. You're just friends. You told me so. That's why I sent for Berenice.'

'You WHAT?' cried Titus.

'And it was a good thing you did,' came a woman's voice from the doorway. 'Now I finally know the truth.'

Jonathan turned his head. A dozen people had gathered in the corridor, no doubt attracted by the Emperor's shouts. Three guards, the two long-haired slave-boys and Titus's steward Agathus. Flavia, Nubia and Lupus were there, too; they must have followed him. And standing in front of this small crowd, filling the doorway, were his uncle Simeon and a woman in a green silk stola. The woman folded her arms and gave Titus a withering look.

'I see I was correct all along,' she said coldly. 'Now I know why you won't have me back.'

'Dear Jupiter!' cried Titus, and his faced drained of colour. 'Berenice!'

SCROLL XXV

Jonathan knew the woman who stood in the open doorway was at least fifty years old, but she looked half that age. As Berenice stepped forward he saw that her eyes – exotically outlined in black kohl – were as green as the emeralds at her throat.

'So Titus,' said Berenice, lifting her chin, 'is this why you summoned me? To publicly humiliate me? I invest ten years of my life in you and now you discard me for a younger version! Again!' She glared at Delilah who ran to hide behind the loom.

'I . . . you . . . I didn't summon you,' spluttered the Emperor. 'What gave you that idea?'

'This letter, stamped with your seal.' She extended a folded piece of papyrus.

Jonathan's stomach flipped and he took a step backwards.

'No,' he muttered to himself. 'It's not supposed to happen like this.'

Titus was studying the letter. 'I don't recognise this handwriting. This letter was not penned by any of my scribes.'

Jonathan took another step back.

Titus turned the parchment over to examine the broken wax disc which had sealed it. 'This seal is mine . . . but it's old . . . not one I use any more. Though I have seen it recently.'

Suddenly he turned his head to look at Jonathan.

'You!' he said between clenched teeth. He moved to Jonathan, grasped his wrist and wrenched it towards him. 'There! The ring I gave you last year. It was you who sent this letter to Berenice, wasn't it?'

Jonathan nodded. He felt sick.

'How?' said Titus. 'How did you know where she could be reached?'

'I knew,' said Simeon, moving into the room. 'Jonathan sent the letter to me and I took it on to her last known address, in Brundisium. His plan made sense to me.'

Titus rounded on Jonathan.

'So this was your plan?'

Jonathan nodded again and gazed at the floor.

'Just as it was your plan,' continued Titus, 'that I summon your father to Rome?'

'Jonathan! Is this true?' His father's voice.

Jonathan could not bring himself to look at his father. 'Yes, father. It's true.'

'You meddling fool!' said Titus through clenched teeth. 'Do you realise what you've done! By the gods! I should . . .'

Jonathan glanced up at his parents, praying that they at least would understand.

But there was only disappointment in his father's face, and betrayal in his mother's eyes.

'Get out!' Titus commanded Jonathan, his face as red

as his cloak. 'Out of this room! Out of my palace! Out of my city!'

Jonathan turned and ran through the double doors, shouldering aside one of the long-haired boys, past his friends' wide-eyed stares, towards a flight of marble stairs.

And as he fled – already feeling the tightening in his chest – he heard Titus's voice echoing along the marble corridor behind him. 'That goes for the rest of you! Get out of my city and never come back!'

Half-blinded by tears and gasping for breath, Jonathan stumbled through the crowded streets of Rome, not caring where his feet took him. Presently he stopped to catch his breath in a cobbled square. As he stood panting, he gazed at the peeling walls of the tall buildings around him. They were covered with graffiti, mostly Latin obscenities, but he also saw a star of David and some Hebrew slogans. One in particular caught his eye:

THE GREAT BABYLON WILL BE DESTROYED
AND THE BEAST WILL PAY.

Jonathan's chest rose and fell as he tried to fill his lungs. His brand was throbbing. Titus's brand.

'Yes,' he muttered between clenched teeth. 'The Beast will pay.'

Somehow the anger welling up inside loosened his chest so that he was able to breathe more easily. He looked around the square, a square like so many others in Rome.

Against one wall was a sputtering fountain. Three sullen-looking boys sat on the fountain's edge. Nearby, two heavily made-up women leaned against a tavern wall. The togas they wore showed their profession. One of them stared openly at Jonathan and whispered something in her friend's ear. They laughed.

Jonathan quickly looked away, went to the fountain and drank. Ignoring the boys' hostile looks he stood and wiped his mouth with the back of his hand. There was a harsh grating of iron wheel-rims as a grim-faced man pushed a laden handcart across the paving stones. The smell of decomposing corpses was so strong that Jonathan almost retched.

He averted his eyes from the bloated bodies. Rome really was a Babylon. It stank of corruption. He had to get away.

But first he needed to get his bearings; he had no idea where he was. The tenement blocks reared up around him, blocking out much of the bright morning sky. Finally, looking through a gap in two of the buildings, he caught a glimpse of a pink temple high on a hill. It took him a moment to recognise the Temple of Jupiter on the Capitoline Hill; he had never seen it from this angle.

If the Temple of Jupiter was up there, it meant the Palatine was somewhere to his left. He turned and started to retrace his steps. He would have to go back to the palace and get his belongings. His friends and his father would be wondering where he was.

His father. Jonathan's face grew hot at the thought of his father lying on the ground at the Emperor's feet, then rising to turn the other cheek to that bully Titus.

And his mother. Seeing her husband humiliated like that.

What had possessed him to bring his father to his mother without giving them any warning? Without making certain they would be undisturbed?

'Stupid!' he muttered. 'I'm so stupid!'

'I have to agree with you there,' said a voice, and Jonathan found his way suddenly blocked by a boy in a greasy brown tunic. The boy was older than Jonathan – about twelve or thirteen – but his size and build were roughly the same. He spread his lips in a nasty smile that revealed several missing teeth. Jonathan realised he was one of the boys from the fountain. The other two stood behind him.

'Any piggy as plump as you,' said the first boy, looking Jonathan slowly up and down, 'who wanders into our part of town . . . well, they really are stupid. Aren't they, boys?'

SCROLL XXVI

Before Jonathan had time to react, Greasy-tunic kneed him in the stomach. As he doubled over, retching, one of the other boys kicked his feet out from under him. Jonathan landed hard on the paving stones, then gasped as the first one grabbed his wrist and pulled it up so that his shoulder was almost torn from its socket. He tried to find his breath to yell.

'Look at this,' came a sneering voice. 'A ring with a boar on it. A piggy wearing a piggy. Go on piggy: SQUEAL!'

As Jonathan felt the ring being pulled from his finger he balled his hand into a fist, thrust it up, felt the satisfying connection of knuckles on chin.

But his feeble blow enraged the boys and they began to kick Jonathan as he lay on the ground. He tried to summon the anger that allowed him to breathe, but they were not holding back, so he gave into fear and curled up like a hedgehog.

Presently he felt a boot on the side of his head, pressing down, squashing his face onto cold, rough stone. 'Don't fight back, piggy, or we'll give you more than a massage. We'll have to play rough. Understood?'

Jonathan gasped for breath, then cried out as the hobnails dug into his cheekbone.

'I said: UNDERSTOOD?'

Jonathan managed to grunt yes.

The crushing boot withdrew and Jonathan lay sobbing for breath as they roughly stripped him. They pulled the ivory pass and herb pouch from his neck, the rings from his fingers, the belt and money purse from his waist. Then they began to remove his clothes.

'Please God,' the part of him that was not fighting for breath prayed silently. 'Please don't let them take everything.'

Flavia Gemina stood in front of a house on the Caelian Hill near the aqueduct of Claudius. She stared at the sky-blue door set back from the two white plaster columns of the porch. The last time she had turned up at her aunt's house unannounced she had almost been turned away.

Finally, when she felt composed, she took a deep breath, stepped forward and banged the familiar door-knocker: a brass woman's hand holding an apple.

'I'm sure they'll be here,' she said to Nubia, Lupus and Mordecai, and tried to give them a reassuring smile. 'They only leave Rome during the hottest months.'

Presently she heard shuffling footsteps, the grumbling of a bad-tempered door-slave and the clack of the peephole being slid open.

'Miss Flavia?' said Bulbus and she saw his beady eyes light up.

'Oh, Bulbus! I'm so glad to see you. Look! I've brought Nubia and Lupus and Jonathan's father with me. Oh please Bulbus! Let us in! Jonathan's missing and we need a place to stay while we look for him!'

'Sorry Miss Flavia,' said Bulbus gruffly. 'You can't come in. You'd best go away. We've all got the plague.'

'Jonathan? Can you hear me?' A man's voice: low, husky, well-educated. 'Don't flinch so . . . I won't hurt you. Are you all right? Here, put my cloak around you, boy.'

Jonathan blinked up at a concerned face with a big nose and bushy grey eyebrows. He could already feel his right eye swelling shut. 'Agathus?'

'Yes. I saw those boys off. They won't be back any time soon.'

'You couldn't have . . . chased them off . . . five minutes ago?' Jonathan allowed the steward to help him to his feet and wrap a cloak round his bare shoulders. He was still shivering.

'What are you doing in *this* district of town?' Agathus's voice was gruff but not unkind. 'Hasn't anyone told you never to come here without a body-guard? Are you all right, Jonathan?'

'Can't breathe . . . herb pouch gone . . . need *ephedron* . . . get my father . . .'

'The Palatine's too far away. You need help right now. Listen, I have a friend who lives nearby. Let me take you to his room. We'll see to your wounds and find you some clothes.'

Jonathan peered up at him. He still couldn't make his body stop shivering.

'You have . . . a friend . . . who lives . . . in *this* district?'

'Yes,' said Agathus. 'Just down this alley.'

'Great Juno's peacock, it's Miss Flavia.' The dark-eyed young man raised his head from the pillow, then let it drop again.

'Sisyphus, you look terrible!'

'If you can't say anything nice . . .' he coughed, winced, then managed a weak smile.

'Oh Sisyphus!' Flavia laid her head on his chest and gave him as much of a hug as the blankets would allow. 'It's so good to see you again.' Sisyphus, her uncle's secretary, had helped them the previous autumn when Jonathan had first disappeared to Rome.

'Much as I'd like to catch up on gossip—' Sisyphus coughed again '—you must go. We've all got the plague.'

'It's all right,' said Doctor Mordecai, stepping forward. 'Flavia's had the fever. She should be immune.'

'Sisyphus,' cried Flavia, 'Jonathan's missing and we need somewhere to stay while we look for him. This is his father, Doctor Mordecai.'

'Delighted . . . to meet you . . . Hello Nubia . . . Lupus.' Sisyphus attempted a smile and then frowned. 'Jonathan's disappeared again? Shouldn't you be . . . looking for him?'

Mordecai nodded grimly and put his hand on Sisyphus's forehead. 'First tell me: how long have you had this fever?'

'Four days,' Sisyphus coughed, 'maybe five.' He struggled up onto one elbow, spat into a chamber-pot beside the bed and collapsed back onto his pillow.

Mordecai glanced down at the contents of the bowl.

'No blood in your sputum, that's good. How do you feel?'

'Weak. My head hurts when I cough.'

Mordecai pulled back the blankets and rested his head on the young man's chest. 'Breathe,' he commanded. 'Hmmm. That's not too bad at all. I don't understand why you're not up and about. Have you had medical attention?'

Sisyphus nodded. 'The doctor—' he had a coughing fit, spat into the bowl again, and finally managed, 'The doctor has bled us every day. He also prescribed a purge and a fast.'

'Master of the Universe!' Mordecai clenched his jaw. 'Not Diaulus!'

Sisyphus shook his head. 'His partner.'

'No wonder you're weak, if he's been draining you of blood and denying you food. Is this the treatment he prescribed for the whole household?'

Sisyphus nodded again. 'We lost the two little ones. The others all except for Bulbus . . . still in their beds . . .'

Mordecai turned to them. 'Nubia, I want you to go to the kitchen, find the biggest cauldron you can and make some soup. Use vegetables, barley and meat. Any meat you can find, but preferably chicken. Lupus, will you brew a pot of sweet mint tea? If there's no mint in the garden, look in the storeroom. Flavia, you'd better come with me and introduce me to your aunt's family. Let's see if we can't get the members of this household back on their feet.'

Jonathan woke by stages, climbing out of a deep, black, utterly dreamless sleep. His whole body ached, but if he did not move the pain was bearable. Presently he became aware of the straw-filled mattress pressing into his back, the heavy woollen blankets over him, the faint odour of mildew. He also smelled coals on a brazier, stale wine, gall-nut ink and the sickly-sweet odour of a chamber-pot. The light beyond his eyelids told him it was day, a fact confirmed by faint street sounds: people walking, talking, arguing, and a dog's deep monotonous bark. From a room somewhere above him drifted a woman's muffled sobs of grief. And from very close by came the scratching of a pen on papyrus. Someone was in the room with him.

Jonathan carefully lifted his aching head from the pillow and opened his good eye. Agathus sat writing at a small table. He had his back to Jonathan but without turning he said, 'You're awake.'

'Yes.' Jonathan heard his voice come out like a croak. 'What time is it? Did I fall asleep?'

'Yes, you did sleep. It's mid-morning of the first day of the week,' said Agathus, dipping his quill pen.

'The first day . . . ? What happened to the Sabbath?'

Agathus put down his pen and swivelled on the wooden stool to face Jonathan. The room's single window was behind him and his face was shadowed. 'I gave you a sleeping draught. Sleep is one of the best healers, as I'm sure your father has told you. And you obviously needed it; you slept for more than a day.'

'Have you spoken to my father? Have you been back to the palace?' The mattress crunched as Jonathan struggled to sit up. He winced. There was no part of his body not in pain. But at least he could breathe.

'Yes, I went back to the palace yesterday, while you were sleeping. I'm sorry, Jonathan, but I'm afraid your father and friends have gone. They're probably back in Ostia by now.'

SCROLL XXVII

'Flavia.' Senator Cornix sat in his bed, propped up by soft cushions and holding a steaming beaker of mint tea. 'It has been many years. Too many. May I thank you for coming to our rescue at this time? I feel much improved, except for this cough. But your doctor assures me it will clear up if I inhale steam every day. What was the man's name? He told me yesterday but I was still too weak to take it in.'

'His name is Mordecai. He lives next door to us in Ostia.'

'That's a curious name. Where is he? Treating my wife?'

'He'll be back soon. He's out looking for his son, my friend Jonathan.'

'Well, his methods seem to be bringing us all back from the gates of Hades. And I believe he's right about the doctor who treated us.' Flavia's uncle was seized by a coughing fit, and when the coughs subsided he said angrily, 'By Hercules! Fever shouldn't happen in the winter. It's only supposed to happen in the summer. That's why I bought that villa in Tuscany, so that we could leave the city during the dog days.' Flavia saw his jaw clench as he struggled with the emotions he was feeling. 'And now to lose my two babies . . . How is my wife?'

'Aunt Cynthia cries all the time,' said Flavia softly. 'But she's not sick any more.'

Her uncle rested his head against the pillow and closed his eyes.

Flavia gently took the beaker of tea from her uncle's grip and put it on the bedside table. 'Try to sleep now, Uncle Aulus. Nubia and Bulbus are making dinner. You'll feel better after you've slept and had some nice boar stewed in red wine and prunes.'

'My father would never leave Rome without me,' Jonathan said to Agathus.

The old man shrugged. 'The Emperor gave your father a command, and he will have been wise to obey.'

Jonathan groaned. He reached up to rub his right eye, then winced at the pain. The skin around it was swollen and tender, and also slightly greasy.

'In the absence of a doctor,' said Agathus, 'I bathed your cuts in oil and wine and rubbed salve on your bruises. I put a special ointment on your eye. And I got the *ephedron* you asked for.'

'Thank you,' said Jonathan.

'I also bought you a tunic, handkerchief, cloth belt and some sandals. I've folded the clothes and put them at the foot of your bed. If you go out, you'll have to use a blanket as a cloak.'

'Thank you.' Jonathan looked round the cube-like room, with its bare plaster walls, swept floor, table, chair, bed and cupboard. 'Where's your friend? The person who lives here.'

Agathus did not reply.

'It was lucky you found me. Were you coming to visit your friend?'

'Jonathan, I'll be honest with you. There is no friend. And I didn't find you by chance.'

'What?'

'She sent me after you.'

'Who? My mother?'

'No,' said Agathus gently. 'Not your mother.'

'Flavia?'

'No,' said Agathus. 'Berenice.'

'But why would Berenice . . . You!' he cried suddenly. 'You're Berenice's agent!'

Agathus nodded and turned back to the desk. He dipped his pen in the ink pot and resumed writing on a piece of papyrus.

'She sent me a letter last month, you know. From Brundisium. Said she had finally decided to leave Italia and return to her own country. She was to leave as soon as the sailing season began. I was to wait for her word and then I was to go to her.'

He stopped writing and looked up at the small unbarred window. 'I have served Berenice for many years. All those years she stayed with Titus, waiting until he should become Emperor and marry her as he promised. Waiting in vain.'

Agathus turned to look at Jonathan.

'Do you know why she wanted to be Empress? Not because she lusted after power or riches. No. She wanted to help her people. Our people. The children of Israel. She used to say she would be Esther to his Xerxes.'

'The beautiful queen who saved her people,' murmured Jonathan.

Agathus nodded. 'And because Esther was queen, she was able to prevent the evil Haman from wiping out the Jewish race. On that occasion the Jews fought back against those who would exterminate them.'

'The festival of Purim,' said Jonathan, and then, 'but Berenice is not good like Queen Esther. She's wicked. Flavia told me that she and her brother—'

'She is passionate, as well as compassionate,' Agathus interrupted. 'And she can be fiercely jealous. She believed your mother was the only barrier to her becoming Empress. I sent her many assurances that Susannah was not the reason for Titus's change of heart, and I finally succeeded in persuading her to go home.'

Agathus stood and looked down at Jonathan.

'But when Simeon delivered your letter saying that Titus and Susannah were just friends – yes, she showed it to me the night she arrived – when she saw that letter, her suspicions were instantly aroused. I don't know whether she suspected some intrigue, or whether she believed Titus might really want her back, but she immediately abandoned her plans to leave Italia.' He glared at Jonathan from beneath his shaggy eyebrows. 'She had finally accepted the truth, that Titus would never make her his Empress. And then you sent that foolish letter.'

'I'm sorry,' said Jonathan miserably.

'Feeling sorry doesn't help. Make it right.'

'How?'

'Berenice made one error of judgment. Titus is not "Xerxes", the misguided but benevolent ruler. Titus is "Haman", the evil tyrant who would exterminate our people. Do you know he intends to open his new amphitheatre with a hundred days of games?'

'My mother said something about it.'

'Think of it, Jonathan: one hundred days! Do you have any idea where he will get enough gladiators to fight and die daily for more than three months?'

Jonathan's blood ran cold in his veins. 'The Jewish slaves,' he said.

Agathus nodded. 'Correct. The men who have been working on that pagan death pit for the past nine years have been building their own tomb!'

'But . . . Are you sure?'

'Where else will he find a thousand gladiators?'

'Volunteers?'

Agathus snorted. 'He'll need those, too, but no. He will finally exterminate all the Jews he brought back from Jerusalem.'

'What can we do?'

'Help me eliminate Titus. It's the only way. Berenice will never stop loving him while he's alive. But with Titus dead, Berenice will have no more ties here. Then she can finally leave this corrupt city and go home.'

'No. I can't do that.' Jonathan closed his eyes, saw the image of his father and mother embracing, and quickly opened them again.

Agathus pulled his stool closer to Jonathan's bed and sat forward.

'Jonathan, think about it. God has shown his displeasure with Titus. First the volcano, then the blighted harvest, the blood-red sunsets, and now this pestilence. Do you know how many years it has been since the First Temple was destroyed?'

Jonathan nodded. 'Flavia told me: 666, the number of the Beast,' he said, and added, 'according to Josephus.'

'Josephus is correct. We are in the end times, Jonathan. Titus is the Beast, another Nero. He must be eliminated.' Agathus spoke these words calmly, as if he were arguing a point of rhetoric.

Jonathan wished he could close his ears as well as his eyes.

'Jonathan, listen to me. Your mother's life may be in danger. You know that Berenice hired three assassins to have her killed last year?'

'How could I forget?'

'After you foiled their plot, I wrote to her. I informed her that Titus and Susannah were just friends. I assured her that Titus had changed. That he had reformed. That he had renounced Eros to devote himself to the Empire . . . But after what Berenice saw and heard yesterday – Titus's open declaration of love for your mother – I wouldn't be surprised if she tries to poison your mother herself!'

A sudden wave of nausea flooded over Jonathan. He managed to lean out of the bed in time, and he retched a bitter-tasting yellow liquid into the chamber-pot. Then he sank back onto the prickly mattress, trembling, aching, drenched in cold sweat. His head hurt and there was the sour taste of vomit in his mouth.

'Drink this.' Agathus brought a beaker to Jonathan's mouth. The cold water rinsed away some of the bitterness.

'Jonathan,' said Agathus, sitting back on the stool. 'Consider what I am about to say: Titus's death would solve your problem. There would be no reason for Berenice to kill your mother. And there would be nothing to keep your mother here in Rome.'

'Even if I agreed,' said Jonathan slowly, 'how could you . . . we . . . do it, without getting caught?'

Agathus looked up at Jonathan from under his bushy eyebrows. 'Tomorrow is the last day of the Parentalia, when the temples reopen. Titus plans to make a special sacrifice at the Temple of Jupiter Optimus Maximus on the Capitoline Hill. He will beg Jupiter to end this pestilence and show his favour. Tomorrow is also the day before Purim, the festival which celebrates the victory of the Jewish people over Haman and his evil minions. It is the perfect day for us to strike.'

'How will you kill him with the priests and people all around?'

Agathus stood and went to his table. On it was a linen shoulder pouch. He brought the pouch and held it open so that Jonathan could look inside.

'A garland?' said Jonathan.

'A poisoned garland. The poison works subtly, giving the appearance of death by fever. When Titus puts the wreath on his head before he makes the sacrifice, he will be the instrument of his own death. Titus may even fall in the very act of sacrificing the bull. Those people who are superstitious will believe the gods have struck him down, and those who are sceptical will believe he merely has the fever. But in such a time as this, nobody will suspect poison.'

Another image flashed into Jonathan's mind: Titus on his funeral bier, eyes closed, hands folded peacefully across his chest.

'I saw the way your mother looked at your father yesterday,' said Agathus softly. 'Anyone could see she cares for him. If Titus were to die, then his younger brother Domitian would be Emperor. Domitian has no interest in your mother. Just think, Jonathan: your mother would be free to go home. You would be together again. Don't you want that?'

'More than anything,' said Jonathan fiercely. 'Why do you think I wrote those letters?'

'Then you must help me.'

'I can't. It's wrong. It's murder.' He was seized by a coughing fit and Agathus waited until he was quiet.

'Is ridding the world of a tyrant murder? Or is it rather mercy?'

Jonathan lay back on the lumpy pillow and closed his swollen eyes. For a moment he let himself wonder what it might be like if Titus was dead and his mother was home. In his mind's eye he saw his mother and his father standing in the sunny inner garden of their home in Ostia, holding hands and laughing.

He suddenly realised that in his entire life, he had never heard either of his parents laugh.

Hot tears squeezed out from between his eyelids and

although his whole body ached he felt the brand on his arm throb with particular insistence.

'All right.' Jonathan opened his eyes. 'I've come this far. I may as well go the whole way. Tell me what you want me to do.'

SCROLL XXVIII

It was an hour past dusk when Nubia and Flavia finally went to the bedroom in which they were to sleep. Mordecai had returned at sunset – no word of Jonathan's whereabouts – and they had helped him feed and tend all the members of the Cornix household. Now they were exhausted.

As Nubia put her clay oil-lamp down on a narrow shelf, she froze. There was some creature crouching in the dark corner of the bedroom. A small rat? A coiled snake?

She held the flickering lamp before her and took a cautious step towards it.

'What is it, Nubia?' Flavia had been brushing her teeth and she stood still, her tooth-stick poised.

'I am not sure.' Nubia felt braver with Flavia watching. She took another step forward, then relaxed. 'It is nothing. Just a little sandal.' She bent, picked up the object and held it out for Flavia to see. The tiny leather sandal fit easily in the palm of her hand.

'Oh Nubia! It's a baby's sandal. It must have belonged to Aunt Cynthia's youngest child, Marcia. It was probably her first shoe.'

Later, after Flavia had fallen asleep, Nubia lay wrapped in a blanket and her lionskin, clutching the little sandal and weeping. She was thinking of her own baby sister Seyala, whom she would never see again.

A chill wind from the northwest had scoured the air above Rome so that the stars blazed in the sky above. The moon had not yet risen and so the two figures climbing the Capitoline Hill were almost invisible. The lamp horns they carried threw a circle of orange light so dim that only a person with very sharp eyes would have noticed the man and the boy moving up the dark cliff face. They had wrapped rags round their boots and their footsteps were so silent that even the watchdogs in the opulent homes on the lower slopes of the Capitoline Hill did not stir.

At the beginning of the climb every step had been agony for Jonathan. He was still bruised from his beating two days before. But presently the pain faded to a dull overall ache. His right eye was swollen almost shut and by the time they reached the hundredth step he was wheezing.

The Temple of Jupiter Optimus Maximus – Jupiter Best and Greatest – filled the whole sky before him. Behind him an enormous moon was just rising, huge and blood-red. It illuminated the top of the massive building before them with an eerie red light.

Jonathan caught his breath. In this light the temple was an awesome sight. A gaping triangular pediment resting on a forest of massive columns, each thicker than the biggest tree trunk he had ever seen.

As he followed Agathus across level ground, a large black shape loomed before him. The altar, not yet lit by the moon. His fingertips on the long block of cold marble guided him round it and now he saw Agathus up ahead, a dimly-lit shape moving towards the steps which, like the altar, were still shrouded in darkness.

'Agathus,' he whispered and heard the wheezing in his voice. 'Will this really work?'

'Of course.' Agathus turned back to him, a vague shape in the darkness.

'But what if a priest makes the sacrifice instead of Titus? What if someone else puts on the poisoned garland?'

'Is your courage failing you so soon? You disappoint me, Jonathan.'

'No, I'm not afraid. It's just that . . .'

'You're having second thoughts?'

'Maybe.'

'Jonathan, listen: Titus destroyed our people, our capital city, our temple. Berenice humbled herself and waited patiently for ten years, living in hope that he would one day make her Empress so that she could help her people. And what does he do? The moment he gains power he discards her for a younger woman.'

'That's not how it happened,' said Jonathan. 'Everybody knows he wept when he sent Berenice away. It was the senate's orders.'

'The Emperor has found consolation very quickly in your mother's arms.'

'They're just friends, not lovers.'

'Until now. Now, thanks to your letter, Titus has realised what the rest of us suspected all along. He's in love with your mother. And thanks to your letter

Berenice has been publicly humiliated for the third time. You know,' he gave a bitter laugh, 'you really opened a Pandora's box.'

'What did you say?' Jonathan stopped again. 'I opened what?'

'Pandora's box. It's a figure of speech.'

'Titus told you about the prophecy?'

'What prophecy? I only meant that you caused a great deal of trouble for a great many people. That's why you must help me put it right. Come on, boy!'

But Jonathan could not move. He stood trembling between the altar and the temple. He felt as if someone had emptied a jug of snow-chilled water over him.

He suddenly knew who Agathus was.

And what must happen.

And the revelation sent a stab of horror through him. He looked around for Agathus, but the steward was already climbing the temple steps.

Jonathan hurried after him.

'Agathus!' he called. 'Wait!'

'Be quiet, you idiot! If they catch us they'll throw us to the beasts in the arena!' Agathus turned and continued up the steps.

Jonathan followed him in silence but when they reached the top step he wheezed, 'You didn't come all the way up here to kill Titus, did you?'

Agathus turned and looked at Jonathan. The red moon illuminated his face and body so that his grey hair seemed bathed in blood. The pupils of his eyes were black.

'No,' said Agathus. 'I didn't come up here just to kill Titus.'

'What, then?' said Jonathan. His body was shivering, and not just from the night air. 'What have you come to do?'

'I've come to do God's will. Tonight our people will be avenged. Tonight Rome dies!'

SCROLL XXIX

Jonathan felt sick. 'How?' he said. 'How will Rome die?'

Agathus lifted the hollow horn from his candle. 'With fire, of course. A holocaust. A burnt offering. Rome is a tumour on the face of the earth. It must be cauterised, burnt away.'

'Fire,' repeated Jonathan and stared at the lamp horn in his own hand.

'It has to be,' said Agathus. 'And it has to start here, at the Temple of Jupiter, the temple which represents Rome throughout the empire. The temple maintained by Jewish taxes. Taxes which should have gone to the Temple in Jerusalem. Titus burned our Temple and now I will burn his. Proof that the gods are angry with Rome. Perfect justice,' he murmured, turning back towards the middle door. 'Thanks to you. You devised the perfect catalyst. You brought Berenice to her senses at last. I couldn't have organised it better if I'd planned it myself.' Agathus turned his back on Jonathan and moved between the enormous fluted columns, their red vertical stripes black in the pink light of the moon.

'Tonight is the perfect night. The temples are still closed. It is the day before Purim. And if this wind holds, it will carry sparks down onto the forum and the Palatine Hill, igniting the temples of their pagan gods and consuming the palace of the Beast.'

'The Imperial Palace?' Jonathan felt numb. 'But my mother's still there. She'll die!'

Agathus shrugged. 'Then she will die for a good cause. For our cause.'

'Berenice will die!'

'She will have left for Judaea early this morning, while you slept. If God wills it, I will join her there.'

'Agathus, please! You can't do this. Hundreds of our people will die. There are thousands of Jews living in Rome, both free and slaves.'

'Most of them have been warned by now. The others are dying anyway, of the pestilence.'

'You'll die, too!'

'The philosopher Seneca says: "Wherever you look you can find an end to your troubles. The way to freedom is over a cliff. At the bottom of a well. Hanging from the branches of a tree." '

'That's Roman thinking,' said Jonathan. 'That's not what we Jews believe. Only God can take life, because he gives it.'

'Wool fluff!' snorted Agathus. 'Think what our brothers did at Masada seven years ago. Three hundred of the bravest Jews who ever lived. They preferred death to slavery.' Agathus stopped and gestured at one of the massive columns in the porch. 'And what about Samson? He pushed down the columns of a pagan temple and killed more by his death than he did in all his life. If I die, at least I will take many Romans with me.'

Agathus turned and moved towards the central door, its painted design black and pink in the moonlight.

'But I'm no fool,' he said, as he pushed the door. 'As soon as I set the fire I'll run.' The door to the temple opened quietly. 'Tonight is the night before Purim, when our people struck back at those who would exterminate them. If I perish, I perish. But if it is God's will—'

'God's will!' said Jonathan, and followed him into the dimly lit cella. 'How can you talk about . . . ?' He trailed off and his head tipped back as his gaze travelled up the massive cult statue. The image of the seated god Jupiter was as tall as Ostia's town wall. Dimly lit by a few oil-lamps below and hanging rings of candles above, the great bearded head seemed to glare down at them.

'Behold their idol, their loathsome Baal,' said Agathus, and he spat on the floor.

But Jonathan was looking around for something he could use as a weapon against Agathus.

Apart from the enormous cult statue there was very little in the inner chamber.

On the back wall of the cella hung an enormous tapestry, not unlike the one in Berenice's quarters. On either side of the cult statue, right up against the red and white painted walls, were small semicircular tables. Even now, when the temple was officially closed for the Parentalia, candles burned to light the cella. Jonathan could see various sacrificial vessels and implements: a silver jug and flat silver bowl, incense burners, strainers and wreaths. But no knives, axes or anything else resembling a weapon.

Agathus went to one of these tables, removed his linen shoulder bag and carefully let the poisoned wreath slip out so that it lay on top of the others.

Jonathan needed to think, he needed to buy time. 'The great fire fifteen years ago,' he whispered. 'The one that destroyed Rome in the days of Nero. Was that your people, too? I mean our people?'

'No. Though I wish it had been. And I wish they had burned Rome to the ground. If they had, Jerusalem might still be standing.' Agathus folded the linen bag and put it under one arm. Then he extended his lamp horn and moved towards the base of the huge statue. 'There should be a secret door here at the side of the base,' he murmured. 'We'll fill the space with oily rags, wait until Titus and all the priests are at the altar, light it, and leave by the priest's door at the back. It's probably hidden behind that curtain. When the flames take hold it will be as if Jupiter himself started the fire. And if my calculations are correct, it will occur just as Titus is pressing the garland onto his head.'

'Agathus! Vengeance is the Lord's. Not ours. You can't play at being God!'

'You talk to *me* about playing God?' Agathus had found the opening in the base of the cult statue: an almost invisible door which had no handle but swung open when it was pushed. 'You tried to orchestrate not only your parents' reunion, but that of Titus and Berenice! You know as well as I do that sometimes God needs a little help. Now, boy, are you with me or against me?'

'With you,' Jonathan lied.

While Agathus stooped to peer through the door-way, extending his uncovered candle to see inside, Jonathan moved silently back to the small marble table against the wall. The silver libation jug would not make a very effective weapon, but a strong blow might knock Agathus unconscious. He slowly put down his lamp horn and grasped the jug. Maybe he could still prevent the prophecy from coming true.

Agathus had found an amphora of olive oil for replenishing the oil-lamps and some rags used for clean-ing. He had put down his lamp and now he was bending over, pouring the oil onto the heaped rags.

'Good,' he grunted as he poured, 'this is perfect.'

Two silent steps took Jonathan back to the base of the cult statue and before Agathus could turn, he lifted the silver wine jug and brought it down as hard as he could on the back of the man's head.

SCROLL XXX

'Ow!' said Agathus, turning angrily. 'That hurt!'

'Oops!' said Jonathan, and quickly raised the dented jug to hit Agathus again.

Agathus snarled and caught his wrist, held it with an iron grip, then began to twist Jonathan's entire arm.

Jonathan cried out and felt his knees bend. The silver jug clattered to the floor. Agathus still held the heavy amphora in his right hand. Before Jonathan was brought to his knees, he instinctively used his downward motion to lunge forward and butt Agathus in the stomach with his head.

'Oof!' cried Agathus, and as his grip loosened slightly, Jonathan sliced his left arm round and hit him as hard as he could in the back of the knees. It was a trick Lupus had taught him. And it worked. As if his legs had been cut from under him, Agathus went down with a grunt, losing his grip on both Jonathan and the amphora. The big clay jug rolled away in a grinding semi-circle and Jonathan heard the thick oil gurgling onto the marble floor.

Jonathan struggled to his feet, lunged for the silver jug, grasped it and turned to strike Agathus again. But that iron grip clasped his ankle and Jonathan felt his foot jerked from underneath him.

The marble floor came up fast, struck him hard in the chest, knocking the air from his lungs and the silver jug from his hand. Jonathan saw his only weapon spin across the marble floor and heard it clatter against the base of the huge statue.

He fought for breath, cursing his feeble lungs for the thousandth time

Agathus loomed over him, glaring down from under his bushy eyebrows.

'You foolish boy. Didn't you wonder why I brought you up here with me? Berenice has finally vowed revenge on Rome, Titus and your mother. She wanted you to be the instrument of your mother's death. And to live with the knowledge of it.'

Jonathan raised himself up on his elbows and stared up at Agathus in horror.

The old man pulled a knife from his waistband.

'And my mistress told me that if you resisted,' he said grimly, 'I was to kill you myself!'

Nubia dreamt that Jonathan was lost in a desert.

Ever since the night the four of them had swum with dolphins, Nubia had felt a bond deeper than friendship with Flavia and the boys.

And deep in her dream she sensed that Jonathan was in fear of his life.

She tried to wake up so that she could tell Flavia, but her eyelids were too heavy. The sun in the dream-desert was beating down on her with such ferocity that she feared her blood would boil.

She tried to call to Jonathan, to tell him to come back

to his friends. Together they could find the oasis. And cool shade. And water. But without each other they would die.

Jonathan writhed away from the swiftly flashing knife and kicked out with his legs. With a terrible ringing noise, the knife struck the marble floor inches from where his chest had been a moment before. This was no game. His heart was pounding so hard he thought it would burst his ribs. He pulled himself wildly across the floor, terror squeezing his chest.

Some instinct told him Agathus was about to strike again, so he rolled away and this time found himself by one of the small tables. Grasping its curved marble edge, he hastily tried to pull himself up. But the table toppled over and Jonathan fell down with it.

Agathus jumped back as silver dishes and oil-lamps crashed to the floor, the sound echoing in the vast space above them. One of the wicks was still alight and a pool of oil on the marble floor suddenly flared up yellow. A flame snaked across the marble floor and ignited the rags Agathus had been soaking a few moments earlier.

Agathus took a step towards Jonathan and his cloth-wrapped shoe flew out from under him. He had slipped in the growing pool of olive oil.

As Jonathan rose to his feet he saw a tongue of fire flicker towards Agathus who was up on his elbows now, staring in horror at the flames, and scrabbling backwards, trying to get away.

He did not see the burning rags behind him. They

ignited his sleeve and at the same instant flames licked the hem of his long tunic.

'Help me!' Agathus screamed. 'Help me!'

He tried to tear away his flaming cloak, but now his tunic was on fire too.

Jonathan stood gasping for air and watching helplessly as Agathus ran towards the curtain at the back of the cella. The screaming man tried to pull it down, tried to smother the flames. But he only succeeded in setting the curtain on fire and now Jonathan saw the flames leap up and up to illuminate the hollow ceiling of the temple.

Jonathan turned and ran out of the cella, through the forest of columns and down the temple steps.

'Help!' he tried to cry, but it only came out as a wheeze. 'Fire!'

At the foot of the dark steps he tripped and fell. Sobbing for breath, he struggled to his hands and knees, then slowly looked up to see a figure moving down the steps after him. A figure engulfed in flames.

Jonathan rose, turned and stumbled through the darkness. As he veered to avoid the dark shape of the altar he collided with a man in a long tunic. It was the priest or one of his assistants.

'Fire!' gasped Jonathan, pointing. 'Fire!'

Now other people were coming, one of them with a leather bucket of water, another shouting at Jonathan to 'Get the vigiles! Quickly! At the bottom of the hill.'

Jonathan nodded, started towards the steps, then turned to look back. The central door of the temple was a dim glow with dark shapes moving in and out.

The priests were wholly intent on saving their god and his temple.

And so that last terrible sight was Jonathan's alone: the sight of a man in flames staggering to the cliff edge and stepping deliberately over.

SCROLL XXXI

The deep clanging of a gong on the hill behind him had alerted the vigiles and Jonathan met them halfway. They wore thick tunics and heavy boots and brandished ladders and spades, leather buckets, and heavy woven mats for beating out fires. There were so many of them coming up the steps that Jonathan had no choice but to turn and let himself be carried back up the hill with them. As the firemen ascended they were joined by others. A senator from one of the houses on the lower slopes, side by side with three of his slaves. Two cart-drivers who had just entered the River Gate and had abandoned their animals and cargoes to help.

Others heard and came to help and so a growing crowd of them swarmed up the hill.

Although no more than ten minutes could have passed, when he reached the summit again Jonathan saw the temple's central door was a brilliant yellow rectangle. The flames inside were burning fiercely.

Suddenly something attacked the lead fireman. Something that hissed and flapped. The big man screamed and staggered back. 'It bit me!' he cried.

Then there was another, and another. Their flapping wings created a breeze Jonathan could feel on his face and their honking filled the night air.

'By all the gods!' cursed one of the firemen. 'It's the sacred geese!'

'Drive them back, man! We've got to put out that fire before all of Rome burns!'

'I can't touch them! They're sacred.'

'Stuff that!' growled a burly man and stepped forward into the geese. There was a crack among the honking and he screamed. 'My arm! It broke my arm!'

'Give me your torch!' cried someone and swung a fiery arc towards the geese. But Rome's protectors were brave birds and by the time the geese had retreated, the sky above the temple was orange. It was obvious even to Jonathan that a few buckets of water and woven mats would not douse this fire.

'Not again!' one of the older vigiles muttered to his friend. 'They only just finished rebuilding it after the last fire.'

'Men!' cried their leader. 'The fire's taken hold. We might as well try to put it out by spitting on it. We have to stop it spreading to the other temples now!'

'It's too late, sir!' One of the vigiles pointed to where three poplar trees had burst into flame. Sparks from the burning temple must have reached them. Above the fire's angry roar Jonathan heard a huge crash. The roof of the temple slowly collapsed and a fountain of flames gushed up, licking at the black heavens and throwing up sparks and drops of fire.

The chief firefighter shouted above the roar. 'Men! The wind shifted half an hour ago. It's coming from the southeast! We have to warn people to the north of the city. Down! Go back down! Warn those who live near the Saepta, the Campus Martius, the Subura and the theatre district. Bang on doors, shout in the streets, tell people to douse their roofs with water. Other vigiles should be alerted by now but they'll need your help. And may the gods preserve us!'

'Nubia? Wake up! Were you having a bad dream? Nubia? Oh no, you're burning up . . . Doctor Morde-cai, Doctor Mordecai. Help! Come quickly! Nubia's eyes look strange. And I don't think she knows who I am!'

When Jonathan and the firemen reached the bottom of the Capitoline Hill they saw what they had feared.

At least a dozen buildings at its base were already ablaze, two of them tall apartment blocks.

People had emerged from their homes and were running to and from the street fountains with buckets of water. Others were hurriedly packing their belongings onto carts. The cinders and sparks floating down from the temple were taking hold.

The firemen pounded through the streets of Rome, banging on doors and shouting warnings. The warm wind moaned in the eves and roof-tiles above them. Then someone found a trumpet and its piercing blare woke the dogs of Rome. Somewhere a donkey was braying and roosters began to crow. Everywhere people screamed and shouted.

But soon another sound drowned out the moaning wind and blaring trumpets and barking dogs. It was the thunderous, incessant roar of the fire which had taken hold and which now threatened to devour Rome.

Lupus found Nubia sitting up in bed. She was looking around the dark room in terror and crying out in a strange language.

As Mordecai rose from her bedside, the flickering lamplight threw his huge trembling shadow onto the wall of the room.

There was a look of deep concern on his face, and Flavia – hovering nearby – was in tears.

'She's burning up with fever,' said Mordecai. 'I don't think she recognises us.'

'What can we do?' cried Flavia.

'I think I must make her vomit,' said Mordecai. 'Lupus, bring my medical bag. It's in my room by my bed.'

Lupus nodded, sprinted across the courtyard and was back a moment later. He had brought a clean chamber-pot with him.

'Good thinking,' said Mordecai. Lupus held the lamp close while the doctor rummaged in his bag, then measured out a draft. Flavia sat on Nubia's bed, holding her friend's hand.

But Nubia showed no sign of recognition. She stared at Flavia in terror, then cried out pitifully in her own language.

'Doctor Mordecai, please!' whimpered Flavia. 'Help her!'

'Drink this,' said Mordecai. He bent over Nubia but she shrank back in terror as his shadow fell across her.

'Here, let me!' Lupus heard Flavia whisper soothing words, as she sometimes did to Scuto, and saw her gently bring the beaker to Nubia's mouth.

Nubia sipped, then coughed and spat out the liquid.

But Flavia persisted and Nubia drank.

Suddenly Nubia bent forward and began to be sick.

Lupus was at the bedside in an instant, holding the bowl out to catch the vomit.

Flavia held her friend's head steady while Lupus gazed in dismay at the liquid pouring into the bowl. It was black.

Presently Nubia finished heaving and lay back on the pillow, her face beaded with sweat.

Flavia mopped her friend's forehead with a cool cloth and presently Nubia opened her eyes. 'Flavia?' she whispered. 'Lupus?'

Flavia sobbed and threw her arms round Nubia's neck.

'There, there,' said Mordecai. 'Don't choke her. She'll be fine now but she needs to sleep.'

Lupus caught Flavia's hand and tugged. He needed to show her something important. She rounded on him but something in his expression must have warned her, for she looked up at Mordecai.

'She'll be all right,' said Jonathan's father wearily. 'Look, she's already asleep.'

Flavia gave her sleeping friend a yearning look but followed Lupus out of the bedroom. Still holding her hand he led her to the iron frame of an ivy-covered pergola. He clambered up it and from there onto the roof. He glanced back once and grunted when he saw that she was still following him.

Presently they straddled the heavy, curved tiles on the apex of the roof; from here they could look out over almost all of Rome. Lupus pointed in the direction of the Palatine Hill.

In the garden of the house next door a cock crowed, convinced that dawn was breaking. Lupus knew Flavia had made the same mistake because she frowned.

'The sun shouldn't be rising over there,' she said, 'that's the west . . .' And then he saw that she understood, for she turned her horrified eyes on him.

'It's not the sunrise,' she exclaimed. 'It's fire! Rome's on fire!'

Of the hour that followed Jonathan remembered only snatches.

He remembered banging on doors, crying out warnings, trying to breathe. People ran down the narrow streets, their shadows thrown before them by the lurid glow of the fire that lit the sky. One family ran past with their hands pressed over their ears to shut out the terrible roar. Two slave-girls carried their sick mistress on a pallet and a young man bore an old man on his back. Jonathan saw a pigeon take flight with its wings on fire.

The floating threads of black soot reminded him of Vesuvius, and he suddenly knew what he must do. Stopping at a crowded street fountain he managed to soak his handkerchief before he was jostled aside. He tied it over his face, so that it covered his nose and mouth. The water in the fountain was warm from the drops of fire that fell hissing into it, so he pushed forward again and splashed himself until he was soaking wet.

Someone screamed in his ear, and he turned to see a wall of fire rearing up over the roofs of the tenement houses and then breaking like a wave, the flames rushing like water through the narrow streets. He ran with the masses in a blind panic, until he saw an old man trampled underfoot. Then he broke away from the crowd and turned down a dark, narrow alley. But a tongue of flame pursued him, as if it had a mind of its own, following whether he swerved right or left and only withdrawing when he stumbled and fell headlong. Sobbing with relief Jonathan struggled to his feet and ran on.

Smoke filled the streets now, and although he wanted to drink great gulps of air his lungs received only sips. Jonathan knew he would not survive without his medicine. So he turned and stumbled in the direction of the nearest place where he could be sure of finding *ephedron*. Towards the Tiber, and Snake Island.

SCROLL XXXII

For three days the fire burned, entirely consuming the Temple of Jupiter Optimus Maximus and all the temples around it. Below and to the north of the Captoline Hill, the fire also destroyed the temples of Neptune, Serapis and Isis, together with the Pantheon, the Saepta, the Baths of Agrippa, the theatres of Balbus and Pompey. It consumed so many sacred buildings that the rumour spread: the disaster must have been caused by one of the gods.

'Boy! Wake up!' said a man's voice in a harsh whisper. 'You don't want to scream like that; you'll frighten the little ones.'

Jonathan opened his eyes to see a strange face peering into his. He had been having a terrible nightmare. His heart was pounding and his body covered in sweat. He lifted his head from the hard pallet and looked around. His scalp felt cold.

It was night and he was in a courtyard full of sleeping figures, many of them children. Dark columns surrounded the courtyard and flickering torches showed a statue at its centre: a statue of a bearded god with a staff.

'Were you dreaming about the fire?' asked the priest,

with a tired smile. 'It's over now. It's almost under control.'

Jonathan reached up to touch his head. It felt strange. His fingertips encountered stubble.

'We had to shave your head,' said the priest. 'Some of the children we've taken in have head lice. It's the only way to contain it.'

'Where am I?' asked Jonathan, his heartbeat slowing to normal.

'You're in the abaton of Aesculapius. The dream-court. We've had to take in the overflow, and we've let the children stay here. There's nowhere else for people to go.'

Of course, thought Jonathan, and let his shorn head drop back onto the straw pallet. The dream-court. The place where sick people come to sleep so that the god can visit them in their dreams, taking the form of a bearded man or a snake to heal them of their diseases.

Abruptly he remembered the nightmare that had made him cry out.

In his dream he had not seen Aesculapius or a snake or a dog.

He had seen his mother holding a clay jar in her hand. A jar with a garland of flowers painted on it. A poisoned garland like the one Agathus had prepared for Titus.

In the dream, his mother had lifted the jar to her lips and drained it. Then the bottle had slipped from her fingers and she had fallen slowly to the ground.

Jonathan knew with a terrible certainty that the dream was true.

His mother had drunk his potion and now she was dead.

'He's not here,' said Flavia, 'and this was the last place on our list. I thought I was so clever, using our imperial passes to get in, but now . . . I can't think where else to look.'

She and Lupus stood in the middle of Berenice's bedroom and stared around. The room had been stripped of everything apart from the bed's wooden frame.

'It looks like she's really left this time,' said Flavia and Lupus nodded his agreement.

SHE EVEN TOOK THE ARK he wrote on his tablet.

'If it really *was* the ark of the covenant,' said Flavia. 'It was probably just her clothes box. Maybe she won't try to kill Jonathan's mother any more now.'

'Haven't you heard?' said a little girl's voice behind them.

'Rizpah!' Flavia cried. 'We thought you had the fever!'

'I did. But I'm better.'

The little girl didn't look better to Flavia; she looked terrible. Her skin was so translucent that Flavia could almost see the veins running beneath it. And there were dark smudges under her eyes.

'Rizpah, Jonathan's missing. Have you seen him?'

'No,' said Rizpah. 'When did you last see him?'

'Not since before the fire.'

'Then he must have heard the news and run away,' said Rizpah, her pink eyes filling with tears.

'What news? What are you talking about, Rizpah?'

'His uncle Simeon is dead. He died of the fever last night.'

'Oh!' cried Flavia. 'Poor Jonathan. He loved his uncle.'

'Simeon was kind to me,' said Rizpah miserably. 'And he was going to be my stepfather. But that's not all.' She looked up at them with eyes even redder than usual. 'Jonathan's mother is dead, too.'

Flavia looked at Lupus in horror, unable to speak, and then back at Rizpah.

Rizpah tried to keep her voice steady as she said, 'Titus says the fever took her, too, but everyone is whispering that she was poisoned.'

'Please,' said Jonathan to the guard at the slaves' entrance of the Imperial Palace.

He stood in the familiar porch with its marble benches and columns, but he did not see any of it.

'I need to get in,' said Jonathan to the guard. 'I may look like a beggar but I promise you I know the Emperor. I want to see if . . . everybody's all right. I have to tell the Emperor some important news.'

The guard laughed. 'Even if I did believe your story – and I don't – the Emperor isn't here. He's gone with the funeral procession.'

'Funeral procession?'

The guard nodded. 'His girlfriend. The Jewess. She

died three days ago, the day the fire started. It's supposed to be a secret, but everyone knows.'

'Berenice?' Jonathan managed to say. 'Berenice is dead?' And he silently prayed: Please let it be Berenice.

'Not her. She's gone home. It was the other one. Susannah, I think her name was.'

Jonathan stared at him, and although he had already known it, a cold numbness began to spread outwards from his heart.

'Rumour is,' the guard leaned forward, 'that she didn't even die of the fever.'

The guard must have taken Jonathan's stupefied look for interest.

'The doctors say,' he continued in an exaggerated whisper, 'that she was murdered. A poison that made it *look* as if she had the plague. What will they think of next?' he said, shaking his head. 'What will they think of next?'

SCROLL XXXIII

'This is terrible,' whispered Flavia. 'Why did we ever come to Rome?'

They were back at Senator Cornix's house on the Caelian Hill. Flavia and Lupus and the senator's eldest son Aulus were sitting beside Nubia's bed. It was noon, and the sky above the courtyard outside was cold and grey.

'We come to Rome because Jonathan sends a letter,' said Nubia weakly, propped up on her cushions. She had lost weight and her golden eyes looked huge in her face. 'He only wants his mother and father to be together.'

'But now his mother's dead,' said Flavia, 'and his father is grief-stricken, and he's gone . . . maybe even . . .' She looked up at Aulus, her twelve-year old cousin, a thin, serious-looking boy with a long face and brown hair. 'You said your father and Sisyphus have gone to check the names of the dead?'

'Yes.' Aulus was slouched in his chair twiddling a brass stylus. 'But Flavia,' he glanced up at her, then quickly down.

'Yes?'

'Father says there are hundreds of bodies in the Campus Martius too badly burnt to be identified and that there may be thousands more whose bodies we'll never find because they were completely destroyed by the flames. Even if Jonathan is dead, we might never—'

Lupus slammed a wax tablet onto the bedside table with such force that they all jumped. He glared at Flavia and Aulus for a moment with red-rimmed eyes, then shoved back his chair and went out of the room and across the courtyard towards the front of the house.

Flavia picked up the wax tablet. It was hers, with her notes from their search for Jonathan. She read what Lupus had written at the bottom:

HE'S NOT DEAD
AND I'LL PROVE IT'

Flavia looked at Nubia. 'I should go and help Lupus look for him,' she said. 'If I go now I might be able to catch him. Aulus, will you stay here with Nubia?'

He nodded. 'That's about all I'm fit for,' he said. 'I think I'd pass out before I reached the bottom of the hill.'

Flavia was hurriedly pinning on her blue palla when Bulbus appeared in the bedroom doorway.

'Imperial messenger here, Miss Flavia. He says your presence is required on the Palatine Hill. You, Nubia, Lupus and Doctor Mordecai. The Emperor wants to see you all immediately.'

'Dear God, what have I done?'

Jonathan sat at the foot of the ruined Temple of

Jupiter Optimus Maximus. He rested his head in his hands and stared down at marble steps scorched by the heat of the flames. Behind him lay the great shattered head of Jupiter. It had fallen from its wooden body and rolled out through the central doorway of the cella. Its nose had broken off and its painted eyes gazed impotently out over Rome.

'Dear God,' Jonathan whispered. He dug his fingernails into his cheeks and pulled until it hurt. 'This time it really is my fault. My fault that Agathus died horribly. My fault that all those people died in the fire. My fault that mother is dead. What have I done?'

Presently he saw his hands were wet with blood where he had scratched his cheeks.

Somehow the sight of his own blood calmed him. He lifted his head and looked out over Rome, still smouldering in a thousand places. The dirty yellow sun had retreated behind a grey cloak of clouds, and it was cold now. It was a still day, with no wind, so the threads of smoke from smouldering fires and morning offerings rose straight up into the grey sky.

Grey sky, grey buildings, grey smoke, everything grey except for the blood-red roofs. A cold, grey world which held no promise of hope.

Jonathan stood and wiped his bloody hands on his tunic.

He stared for a moment at the shattered head of Jupiter, twice as tall as he was but just as hopeless.

Slowly he turned and walked towards the Tarpeian Rock. The rock from which they threw traitors. The rock from which Agathus had leapt.

When Jonathan reached the edge he looked down. Below him the rocks were dirty, jagged and ugly. A black and tan raven was picking at something among them.

Standing there on the cliff edge, Jonathan tried to pray. But no words came. If only he had prayed before, on the night of his father's birthday, instead of taking matters into his own hands. Instead of playing God.

As he gazed down at the stomach-churning drop, he suddenly remembered the words Agathus had quoted:

'The way to freedom is over a cliff.'

Then the raven below him cawed its harsh cry: '*Cras! Cras!* Tomorrow! Tomorrow!'

And Jonathan remembered that for Prometheus there was no easy death, but an unending punishment in which each tomorrow brought new torment.

The long-haired slave-boy named Bigtha led Flavia and Mordecai to a part of the Imperial Palace they had never seen before. Presently he scratched at gilded double doors.

'Come,' said a voice and they stepped into the private quarters of the Emperor.

Titus, wearing a white woollen tunic and leather slippers, stood warming his hands over a brazier. He looked up as they entered and Flavia thought his face looked tired, almost thin.

'Doctor Mordecai, thank you for coming. Have you had any news of Jonathan?'

'No.' Mordecai's shoulders slumped. 'I thought perhaps you had.'

'No,' said Titus. 'But I have alerted all my vigiles. We'll find him if he's . . .' The Emperor did not finish his sentence. Instead, he heaved a deep sigh.

'There is some good news,' said Titus. 'In the past day there has not been a single new instance of fever reported. It seems the gods have finally taken pity on us.' He turned to Mordecai. 'I'm so sorry I lost my temper with you last week,' he said. 'It's my headaches. They're getting worse . . . I have decided to take the tonic you recommended.'

'Good,' said Mordecai bleakly.

'And I'm sorry I drove Jonathan away. Afterwards, I . . . My own mother died when I was only a boy. I still remember the terrible ache and how I prayed to the gods. I vowed to give them anything if they would bring her back. How soon we forget what it's like to be a child.' He looked around. 'Where are Lupus and Nubia?'

'Nubia's recovering from the fever,' said Flavia, 'and Lupus is out looking for Jonathan. But we left word at Senator Cornix's house, telling him where we are. In case he gets any news . . .'

'I have something to tell you,' said Titus.

He went to the arched window and stared out through the iron stars which barred it.

For a long moment he was silent. Then he spoke: 'I dislike politics. I hate the games men play, the pretence, the lies. I prefer to say what I think, to charge straight ahead . . . I suppose it's because I'm a soldier at heart, not a politician. But sometimes even honest soldiers need to lie.' He turned back to them.

'Berenice is a passionate, proud and jealous woman. I have wounded her many times, but when I publicly told Susannah I loved her, I believe that was the worst. She has now left Rome – for good, I hope – but I believe she still has an agent somewhere in the palace. Such a proud woman will not forget such an insult. In the past I have not been able to look at a girl without finding she has been banished or branded. Imagine what Berenice would do to Susannah, to whom I professed undying love.'

'My wife is dead,' said Mordecai heavily. 'What can Berenice do to her now?'

'Nothing,' said Titus with a weary smile. 'Nothing at all.' He turned and moved towards a door, rapped on it twice with his knuckles, then turned back to them.

'That is why I had to kill her.'

SCROLL XXXIV

'You!' gasped Flavia. 'You killed Jonathan's mother?'

'In a manner of speaking,' said Titus.

The door behind him opened and a veiled woman moved into the room. The filmy veil was black, like her long stola. Flavia could vaguely see the smudges of eyes and mouth in the face behind, but nothing else.

The woman raised her hands and pulled the veil away from her face.

Flavia gasped.

It was Jonathan's mother.

'Susannah!' Mordecai staggered, reached out, and gripped Flavia's shoulder to steady himself. 'You're alive! But how can this be?'

'At first we thought she had died,' said Titus, taking Susannah's hand. 'But my physician said she was merely in a deep trance, brought on by some draught.' He turned to her. 'You say Jonathan gave it to you?'

Susannah nodded. 'I take it on day Jonathan disappears,' she whispered. 'To help me sleep.' She looked very pale, but even more beautiful than ever, thought Flavia.

'It gave me an idea,' said Titus. 'If Berenice thought Susannah had died and no longer had a hold on me, then she would more readily obey me if I sent her away. My plan worked. Berenice was convinced. She meekly took the last of her possessions and left Rome the day the fire started. My agents say she is back in Brundisium where she will no doubt wait for the beginning of the sailing season. Meanwhile, Susannah should be safe from any acts of revenge as long as Berenice believes her to be dead.'

'And if someone discovers the truth?' said Mordecai, whose eyes had not left Susannah's face. 'In a palace of a hundred slaves and a thousand intrigues . . .'

'That is indeed a problem. If Susannah remains here, even in hiding, there is a very great risk of someone finding out. But that would not happen in Ostia, where no one knows of Susannah's existence.'

Susannah and Mordecai both looked at Titus in surprise.

'That's right,' he said, releasing Susannah's hands. 'I ask you to leave Rome, my dear. You may either return to Ostia with your husband or I will send you to any part of the world you like, give you a new name, a new identity. The decision is yours.'

Susannah looked at Titus with gratitude, bowed her head, then turned to Mordecai, whose eyes had never left her face.

Flavia saw that Jonathan's father was trembling. Once in the forum she had seen a runaway slave standing before his master with the same expression on his face, knowing the man had the power of life or death.

'I will go home with my husband,' said Susannah softly. 'If he will take me back.'

Mordecai closed his eyes for a moment and lifted his face to the ceiling. Then he nodded at Susannah and held out his hand. She moved to take it, and they embraced.

As Flavia watched them she felt a strange tightness rise up in her throat – a complex mixture of joy and sadness. Her vision blurred as tears filled her eyes.

'Oh, Jonathan!' she whispered to herself. 'Why aren't you here to see this?'

Mordecai and Susannah were still holding hands and talking to one another in low tones when there came a soft scratching at the door.

'Quickly, Susannah!' said Titus in a low, urgent voice. 'Get back in the inner room. Nobody must know you are still alive.' He waited until the door closed behind her. Then he said, 'Come!'

Lupus stepped into the room, his ash-smudged face streaked with tears. Ascletario the astrologer was close behind him.

Lupus moved slowly towards them and opened his hands as if he were bringing an offering to some shrine.

Mordecai took the scorched rings with a cry and Flavia felt a chill of recognition. Although they were blackened she saw that one had a gem inscribed with a boar. The other was set with a ruby.

Flavia knew the rings belonged to Jonathan.

'Please to note . . .' said Ascletario, 'there is a rumour that a boy set the fire at the Temple of Jupiter.'

'A boy?' Flavia whispered.

Ascletario nodded his narrow head. 'A boy with dark

curly hair and a bruised face. The priests saw him running away afterwards, as the fire took hold.'

'Then he might still be alive?' asked Mordecai in a voice hardly more than a whisper.

Ascletario shook his head.

Flavia swallowed hard; her throat felt too tight.

Ascletario continued, 'The priests on Snake Island . . . someone brought them a boy's body – not recognisable. And please to note . . . please to . . .' Tears began to run down Ascletario's thin cheeks. He covered his face with his hands and his thin shoulders shook.

Lupus's hand was trembling but he wrote with grim determination on his wax tablet. Then he held it up for them to see:

THEY FOUND RINGS ON BODY.
IT MUST BE JONATHAN.

*

As an imperial scribe mounted the rostra in the forum, a crowd began to gather. Soon there were hundreds of faces gazing expectantly up at him.

A greasy rain had doused any smouldering fires but the stench of scorched wood and burnt flesh still hung over the city. The paving stones of the forum were cold and slippery.

'Going to tell us who set the fire?' cried a bald butcher in a bloodstained apron.

'Will we get compensation?' shouted a woman with dyed yellow hair and a powdered white face.

The scribe looked around impassively and waited. Presently, when the crowd grew silent, he unrolled the parchment and read in a voice trained to carry across a crowded battlefield:

'Romans and Foreigners! Patricians and Equestrians! Plebs, Freedmen and Slaves! Hear this message of our first citizen Titus Flavius Vespasian. Our illustrious Caesar will hold funeral games for his father in one month. He will sponsor the most spectacular show ever known, a sacrifice of blood to appease the wrath of the gods. These games will last one hundred days and there will be gladiatorial fights on every one of those days.'

There was a scattered cheer from the crowd. Here was something to take their mind off their troubles: free games, lasting over three months.

'Our illustrious Caesar,' the herald was saying, 'therefore invites all those who would fight in the arena to register now. Volunteers will receive room, board and training in the new gladiator quarters. Most of you who volunteer will die. But it will be a noble death, spilling your blood to honour the divine Vespasian. And,' here he paused for effect, 'those few who survive the games will receive a wooden sword to mark their freedom and a purse of gold to start a new life.'

These last words won him a heartier cheer.

'I repeat,' said the messenger. 'Most of you will die. And once you enrol, you lose your identity. Present yourself to the scribe sitting at this table here below me and choose a name for yourself. Once you have told him your new name, you will immediately be taken to the new School of Gladiators. There you will undergo intensive training until the games. May the gods be with you. That is all.'

Already a queue had formed: muscular young men, laughing and boasting and pretending not to be scared. A good number of slaves followed them, some young, some old, two of them women.

A boy joined the end of this group. He was husky, with a shaved head, scratched cheeks and a black eye. He wore sandals a size too big and a torn grey tunic.

Presently he stood before the table. The scribe looked up at him and hesitated. 'You're far too young to enlist,' he said. 'Freeborn males have to be at least twenty-five.'

The boy lifted the sleeve of his tunic to show them the brand on his left shoulder.

The scribe exchanged a glance with the lanista, who stood beside him.

'The Emperor said amnesty for all slaves,' said the lanista in Thracian, his mother tongue. 'The law doesn't apply to them.'

'And he's got the right build,' replied the scribe, in the same dialect.

'He does indeed,' said the lanista with a laugh. 'And it might amuse the crowds to see such a young one fight. Take his name.'

The scribe nodded and looked up at the boy.

'Name?' he said in Latin. 'Have you chosen your new name?'

Jonathan nodded.

'Prometheus,' he said. 'Call me Prometheus.'

FINIS

ARISTO'S SCROLL

abaton (*ab*-at-on)
> holiest part of a sacred area; in the sanctuaries of Aesculapius it was set aside for sleep-cures and prophetic dreams

Aeneas (uh-*nee*-uss)
> Trojan son of the goddess Venus who escaped from conquered Troy to have many adventures and finally settle near the future site of Rome

Aeneid (uh-*nee*-id)
> Vigil's epic poem about Aeneas (see above)

Aeschylus (*ess*-kill-us)
> Perhaps the most famous Greek tragedian; he flourished in the fifth century BC

Aesculapius (eye-*skew*-*lape*-ee-uss)
> Greek Asklepios: son of Apollo and Coronis, he was the god of healing; his main cult centre was Epidauros in Greece and the snake was his special animal

Alexandria (al-ex-*and*-ree-ah)
> port of Egypt and one of the greatest cities of the ancient world

amphitheatre (*am*-fee-theatre)
> an oval-shaped stadium for watching gladiator shows, beast fights and executions. The Flavian amphitheatre in Rome (the 'Colosseum') is the most famous one

amphora (*am*-for-uh)

    large clay storage jar for holding wine, oil or grain

Apollodorus (uh-pol-uh-*dor*-uss)

    Greek author who wrote an account of the Greek myths

Asclepiades (uh-skleep-ee-*ah*-dees)

    Greek doctor of the first century BC whose diet therapy made him popular

atrium (*eh*-tree-um)

    the reception room in larger Roman homes, often with skylight and pool

Av

    month of the Jewish year roughly corresponding with July/August; the First and Second Temples were destroyed on the ninth day of this month

Baal (*bah*-all)

    a near Eastern storm-god despised by Jews, who worship only one God

barbiton (*bar*-bi-ton)

    a kind of Greek bass lyre, but there is no evidence for a 'Syrian barbiton'

Babylon (*bab*-ill-on)

    ancient city near the Euprates River near modern Baghdad; it became the power centre first of the Babylonians and later of the Persians

Berenice (bare-uh-*neece*)

    a beautiful Jewish Queen, from the family of Herod, aged about 50 when this story takes place

brazier (*bray*-zher)

    coal-filled metal bowl on legs used to heat a room (like an ancient radiator)

Brundisium (brun-*deez*-ee-um)

    important Roman port on the heel of Italy; modern Brindisi

Caelian (*kai*-lee-un)

    one of the seven hills of Rome, site of the Temple of Claudius and many homes

caldarium (kall-*dar*-ee-um)

    hot room of the public baths with a hot plunge pool

Capitoline (*kap*-it-oh-line)

    the Roman hill with the great Temple of Jupiter at its top; not as impressive today as it would have been in Flavia's time

carruca (ka-*ru*-ka)

    a four-wheeled travelling coach, often covered

Catullus (ka-*tull*-us)

    Roman poet who lived about 140 years before this story takes place; famous for his passionate, witty and often rude poetry

cautery (*caw*-ter-ee)

    the practice of burning living human flesh for medical purposes

cella (*sell*-uh)

    inner room of a temple which usually housed a cult statue

ceramic (sir-*am*-ik)

    clay which has been fired in a kiln, very hard and smooth

Cerberus (*sir*-burr-uss)

    three-headed mythological hellhound who guards the gates of the Underworld

Circus Maximus (*sir*-kuss *max*-i-muss)

    long race-course in the centre of Rome, at the western foot of the Palatine Hill

Claudius (*klaw*-dee-uss)

the fourth emperor of Rome; he ruled from AD 41 to AD 54

colonnade (call-a-*nade*)

a covered walkway lined with columns

compluvium (com-*ploo*-vee-um)

skylight in the atrium above the impluvium (rainwater pool)

Corinth (*kor*-inth)

Greek port town with a large Jewish population

Cumae (*cue*-my)

home of the Sybil near the Bay of Naples

Dido (*die*-doe)

Queen of Carthage in North Africa who loved Aeneas so much that she killed herself when he left her

domina (*dom*-in-ah)

a Latin word which means 'mistress'; a polite form of address for a woman

Domitian (duh-*mish*-un)

the Emperor Titus's younger brother, 29 when this story takes place

ephedron (*eff*-ed-ron)

a plant mentioned by Pliny the Elder, still used today in the treatment of asthma

Epidauros (ep-id-*ow*-ross)

Greek site of the sanctuary of Asklepios, the healing god

Erasistratus (air-rass-*ist*-rat-uss)

Greek doctor of the third century BC who lived in Alexandria

Esther (*ess*-tur)

beautiful Jewish exile to Babylon who became queen and

saved her people from extinction, according to the book of the Bible named after her

Falernian (fal-*air*-nee-un)

region in Campania widely believed to be the best for wine in Roman times

Faunus (*fawn*-uss)

mysterious woodland god who had a small sanctuary on the Tiber Island

Flavia (*flay*-vee-a)

a name, meaning 'fair-haired'; Flavius is another form of this name

forum (*for*-um)

ancient marketplace and civic centre in Roman towns

freedman (*freed*-man)

a slave who has been granted freedom; his ex-master becomes his patron

frigidarium (frig-id-*ar*-ee-um)

the room of the public baths with the cold plunge pool

garum (*gar*-um)

popular sauce and seasoning made from fermented fish entrails

Haman (*hay*-man)

wicked man who wanted to wipe out the entire Jewish race according to the Biblical book of Esther

Hebrew (*hee*-brew)

holy language of the Old Testament, spoken by (religious) Jews in the first century

Hesiod (*heess*-ee-odd)

one of the most ancient Greek poets; he wrote poems about the creation of the world, the origin of the gods, and how to live

Hippocrates (hip-*pock*-rat-eez)
> a famous Greek doctor who lived in the fifth century BC; often called 'the father of medicine'

hubris (*hyoo*-briss)
> Greek word for massive pride or arrogance, especially in defying the gods

humours
> the theory of the 'four humours' was developed by the Greek doctor Hippocrates

hydromel (*hi*-dro-mel)
> honey-water, a drink often prescribed to those who were ill

Ides (eyedz)
> thirteenth day of most months in the Roman calendar (including February); in March, May, July and October, the Ides occur on the fifteenth day of the month

Josephus (jo-*see*-fuss)
> ewish commander who surrendered to Vespasian, became Titus's freedman and wrote *The Jewish War*, an account of the Jewish revolt in seven volumes

Judaea (jew-*dee*-uh)
> ancient province of the Roman Empire; modern Israel

Juno (*jew*-no)
> queen of the Roman gods and wife of the god Jupiter

Jupiter (*jew*-pit-er)
> king of the Roman gods; together with his wife Juno and daughter Minerva he forms the Capitoline triad, the three main deities of Rome

Kalends (*kal*-ends)
> the Kalends mark the first day of the month in the Roman calendar

kohl (kole)
> dark powder used to darken eyelids or outline eyes

laconicum (luh-*con*-i-kum)

the hottest room in the Roman baths; the small laconicum had dry heat

lanista (la-*niss*-tuh)

the man who trains gladiators to fight in the arena

lararium (lar-*ar*-ee-um)

household shrine, often a chest with a miniature temple on top, sometimes a niche

Leto (*lee*-toe)

the divine mother of Apollo and Diana

Lupercalia (loo-purr-*kal*-ya)

a festival of purification and fertility on the Ides of February; two noble-born youths smeared with goat's blood would run half naked through Rome, striking people with bloody strips of the sacrificed goat to make them fertile

Masada (m'-*sod*-uh)

Judean fortress which held out against besieging Roman legions for many months; finally in AD 73 the Jewish defenders committed suicide rather than surrender

memento mori (m'-*men*-to *more*-ee)

Latin for 'reminder of death' or 'remember you will die'

Messiah (mess-*eye*-uh)

the Hebrew word for Christ; both words mean 'anointed' or 'chosen' one

Minerva (m'-*nerve*-ah)

goddess of wisdom and daughter of Jupiter

minotaur (*mine*-oh-torr)

mythical creature with the body of a man and the head of a bull modus operandi (*mo*-duss op-er-*an*-dee)

> Latin for 'way of operating' or 'method of doing something'

mulsum (*mul*-some)

> honey-sweetened wine most often drunk at the beginning of a meal

Nero (*near*-oh)

> wicked Emperor; built the Golden House after the great fire of Rome in AD 64

Niobe (ny-*oh*-bee)

> mother of seven sons and seven daughters who boasted she was better than Leto, who had only two; her story is a famous warning against hubris

Oedipus (*ed*-ip-uss)

> a hero from Greek tragedy who unknowingly murdered his father and married his mother, then blinded himself when he discovered what he had done

Ostia (*oss*-tee-uh)

> the port of ancient Rome and home town of Flavia and Jonathan ben Mordecai

Ovid (*aw*-vid)

> famous Roman poet who lived about 70 years before this story

Palatine (*pal*-uh-tine)

> one of the seven hills of Rome; the greenest and most pleasant; the site of successive imperial palaces (the word 'palace' comes from 'Palatine')

palla (*pal*-uh)

> a woman's cloak, could also be wrapped round the waist or worn over the head

papyrus (puh-*pie*-russ)

the cheapest writing material, made of pounded Egyptian reeds

Parentalia (pair-en-*tal*-ya)

A nine-day festival from 13 to 21 February in which the living remembered their dead ancestors. The first eight days were for private mourning and the last for public ceremonies. Temples usually closed during this festival

pergola (*purr*-go-luh)

an arbour or walkway made of plants trained to grow over trellis-work

peristyle (*perry*-style)

a columned walkway around an inner garden or court-yard

Perseus (*purr*-syooss)

mythological son of Jupiter and Danae, his task was to get Medusa's head

plebs

the ordinary people, the lowest class of freeborn Romans

Pliny (*plin*-ee)

(the Elder) famous Roman author; died in the eruption of Vesuvius

Pollux

one of the famous twins of Greek mythology

porphyry (*por*-fur-ee)

a type of marble imported from Egypt; red porphyry was a deep burgundy colour evenly sprinkled with pink or white flecks

Purim (*poor*-im)

Jewish festival celebrating Queen Esther's victory over the evil Haman

quotidian fever (quote-*id*-ee-un)
> a fever that continues daily without abating

rostra (*ross*-tra)
> the famous speakers' platform in the Roman forum; it got its name from the prows (rostra) of conquered ships attached to it

Sabbath (*sab*-uth)
> the Jewish day of rest, counted from Friday evening to Saturday evening

Saepta (sigh-ptah)
> a colonnaded area north of the Capitoline Hill in the Campus Martius

scroll (skrole)
> a papyrus or parchment 'book', unrolled from side to side as it was read.

sestercii (sess-*tur*-see)
> more than one sestercius, a brass coin. Four sestercii equal a denarius

shalom (shah-*lome*)
> the Hebrew word for 'peace'; can also mean 'hello' or 'goodbye'

signet ring (*sig*-net ring)
> ring with an image carved in it to be pressed into wax and used as a personal seal

Stabia (sta-*bee*-uh)
> modern Castellammare di Stabia; a town south of Pompeii; also known as Stabiae

stylus (*stile*-us)
> a metal, wood or ivory tool for writing on wax tablets

stola (*stole*-uh)
> a long tunic worn mostly by Roman matrons (married women)

Subura (suh-*burr*-uh)

district of Rome near the Esquiline Hill known to be poor, noisy and dangerous

tac! (tak)

a shortened form of the Latin imperative 'tace' ('be quiet')

Tarpeian (tar-*pay*-un)

a cliff on the Capitoline Hill; traitors were executed by being thrown off it

Titus (*tie*-tuss)

Titus Flavius Vespasianus – aged 40 – was Emperor of Rome in AD 80

toga (*toe*-ga)

a blanket-like outer garment, worn by freeborn men and boys, and by disreputable women

Torah (*tor*-uh)

Hebrew word meaning 'law' or 'instruction'. It can refer to the first five books of the Bible or to the entire Old Testament

triclinium (trick-*lin*-ee-um)

ancient Roman dining room, usually with three couches to recline on

tunic (*tew*-nic)

a piece of clothing like a big T-shirt; children often wore a long-sleeved one

Vespasian (vess-*pay*-zhun)

Roman Emperor who died eight months before this story begins; Titus's father

Vesuvius (vuh-*soo*-vee-yus)

the volcano near Naples which erupted on 24 August AD 79

vigiles (*vig*-ill-aze)

the policemen/firemen of ancient Rome; the word means 'watchmen'

Virgil (*vur*-jill)

a famous Latin poet who died about 60 years before this story takes place

wax tablet

a wax-covered rectangle of wood used for making notes

Xerxes (*zurk*-sees)

King of Persia in the fifth century BC; according to the Bible, the Jewish beauty Esther was one of his queens; later Xerxes fought the Greeks and was defeated

THE LAST SCROLL

We know from at least two Roman historians that there was a plague and fire in Rome in the winter months of AD 80, during the reign of Titus. We don't know much about the plague, but we do know that the fire destroyed the temple of Jupiter Optimus Maximus as well as the sacred buildings around it and the area to the northwest, below the Capitoline Hill.

That much of this story is true.

The rest is made up. There were no such people as Susannah, Agathus, Delilah, Bigtha, Biztha, Simeon, Rizpah or Senator Cornix.

The Emperor Titus was a real person, of course, as was Josephus, the famous Jewish historian under his protection. The beautiful Jewish queen Berenice existed, too. She really was Titus's lover but left Rome shortly after Titus became Emperor. Historians do not know what happened to her after that. There is no evidence that she came back to Rome in AD 80.

However, there is a rumour that Berenice acquired certain holy objects from the great Temple of God in Jerusalem after it was destroyed in AD 70; the curtain of the Temple and perhaps the ark of the covenant, too.

To this day nobody knows what happened to those objects. Or if they do know, they're not telling.